CHAUNS

Where are they now?

ILONA SLACK

Contents

Written and illustrated by Ilona Slack

ISBN-13: 978-1720384151

Printed by CreateSpace

The Find

One fine day whilst filming at dawn,
I stumbled upon a leprechaun!
I aimed for a bee, my camera on zoom,
and saw him sat on top of a bloom.
I could not believe my eyes,
His pointy ears, his tiny size,
they weren't like the myths have told
of bearded men with pot of gold.

He was so deep in thought,
that my presence wasn't caught,
I could take a really good look
As deep breaths he slowly took.
His solemn eyes were bright,
His short slacks quite tight.
He was grey and hard to spot,
even on a close up shot.

I went to greet him with an hello,
But I scared the little fellow.
He hid behind a leaf nearby,
I had a feeling this was goodbye.
I was to go and leave him be,
When he took a peek at me,
I rushed to say "Don't run away!
I want to greet you if I may."

He came closer, nothing to say,
But at least it meant I could stay.
I hoped that we could get on well,
And many stories he would tell.
He saw right through me there,
And then told me with a stern glare,

"I have no stories yet to share.
Tell me a tale, this price is fair."

I thought of one there and then
lucky he didn't ask for ten.
Silly it may be, funny perhaps not,
Sadly one chance was all I'd got.
"Wacky Wind," I blurted out,
a strange title without a doubt.
And so then I began the tale,
that would either win or fail.

Wacky Wind

There was once a planet, and this planet was *Planet Best At*. No one knew for sure what this planet was best at, because the name forgot to include it. Most likely, it was short for Planet Best At Being A Planet To Live On, or so thought the young Wizard of Middlemost, for the lush emerald woods covering large swaths of it enclosed his home and favourite place.

There was no land like his, no forest like his, no house like his, no fun like he could have here, anywhere else. Of this he was very certain, for he knew too well, that the Wacky Wind came from somewhere out there, who was not his friend but a rather frequent visitor despite never being invited. The wizard was supposed to be alone in Middlemost, with no one around to witness or make fun of him for being rather bad at magic.

On this very day too, which was a dark Sunday with chunky clouds nibbling away the top of the trees, the Wacky Wind was already quietly lurking in his thick forest, swiftly dancing around big trunks and rattling autumn leaves. When it stopped playing, and a silent moment swept through the forest, a creaking little door could be heard among the trees. It belonged to the curious house the wizard lived in; the shape of a pointy cupcake sprinkled with leaves and flowers.

Instead of a smoky chimney, there was a peacock fountain gushing water that flowed through the floral roof and turned into foam and bubbles before touching the ground. It vanished so neatly, that it was a mystery even to the wizard how the water never ran dry. Next to the waterfall was a small round window and then the door, which had plates on it, and forks and spoons and even napkins, as if it were the dinner table standing guard.

In the door that was now ajar, the tip of a finger slowly appeared, then a hand reached out until a whole arm and a grumpy face was seen, as the wizard had to make absolute and definite sure that no rain or wind was to spoil his entrée. Being cautious was essential because his unwanted guest was hard to notice. In fact, he never knew for sure whether the Wacky Wind was already there or not.

Feeling somewhat assured, he decided it was safe to step out. He was a bit short so it was not obvious whether or not his coat was meant to reach his knees, but it did. He wore no socks, just a pair of leather slippers with bells inside them, which rang a soft chime as he walked.

His glasses were big and mostly rectangular, but the most unique thing about him was the hat he tied under his chin with strings. I really shouldn't tell, because he intended to keep it a secret, but it was fairly obvious from just looking at it, that this was because the hat was far too small. Not fitting his head very well, he decided to secure it by tying it around his face.

His steps were small and slow, and he took great care in looking ahead, then around before advancing further. The wizard knew very well that knowing when the wind was around meant that he would be in for a surprise. Not knowing whether the wind was around, however, came with the uncertainty that he may or may not be in for a surprise.

It wasn't always like that though. He used to go out without worry, back when Middlemost was not spoilt by the Wacky Wind, which was not a long time ago. Only a week, just one week of tiring, unfortunate tricks the wind played on him made him feel rather worn out. As if being bad at magic wasn't enough, now he also had to find a way to know for sure if the nasty wind was here to meddle, because this could not go on like this he thought.

You see, when it all started on Monday, the morning

was damp with smudgy grey clouds sluggishly passing by. The paths were moist from overnight rain but firm enough to walk on, so the wizard stepped out. But soon he slipped on a large, muddy puddle that formed right in the middle of his pathway. Of course he wouldn't have seen it, as the wind had cleverly covered its surface with fallen autumn leaves.

As the Wacky Wind, perhaps not so graciously, thought this was funny and chuckled, it blew a short, but strong breeze at the wizard, revealing its presence. The wizard did not find the muddy situation funny in the slightest. In fact, he couldn't have found it any less entertaining than he did at that moment. "Go away, nasty wind!" the wizard said as he stood up.

But the wind did not go away and even if it did, it was certainly back on Wednesday as the wizard was to discover, when he was practising how to make a toad stall triple in size. Enlargement magic was hard and he never succeeded with it, but he kept trying because he would have loved to enlarge his hat one day.

He concentrated very hard and directed his palm towards the toad stall as he murmured spells but there was no change. When he decided to try one more time, he closed his eyes to focus very deeply and then opened them as he aimed his spell, but there was a sudden gust of wind and his glasses flew off.

Not seeing much without them, his spell hit a leaping frog instead. The wizard had no chance to be delighted at the success of the spell, because the frog looked terribly frightened at the sudden change in size, and the poor thing disappeared among the trees with just a couple of huge leaps.

Thanks to the wind, now there was a rather large frog somewhere in this forest and he had no chance to find it, unless perhaps by accident. It made him feel bad, so he kept his eyes wide open, hoping one day the frog can be returned to normal, and believing that perhaps now, with a bigger stomach as well, the frog will eat more of those nasty flies that find great joy in entering—but not leaving—his house. That was a rather nice thought, and it cheered him up somewhat.

And you wouldn't believe, just like the wizard hadn't until Friday, when he had to find out for sure, that there are spells for sneezes. An awful lot of them as a matter of fact, since there are no identical sneezes in this world. And trying to sneeze again, an exact kind that sounds just like your last one did to the very last pitch is pretty impossible, isn't it?

Well, making this discovery came at a great price, costing the wizard his one and only treasured cauldron, which was over a thousand years old, and made of the finest metal wizards could find back then. Many, many have used it before him but it didn't show. He had great joy in this cauldron, which always made him think what a fine piece of potion-ware it was with its perfectly rounded bottom. Its lack of legs was no problem as it could hover itself beautifully.

When the wizard took it in the garden hoping to practise magic in the sunshine, the wind blew dust into his face. It was only gentle, but very sudden, so his face turned into a tight sea of wrinkles. A moment later came the most bizarre sneeze that he ever sneezed. It was long with a rising pitch at the end. Starting with a sharp and short *"hat"* and ending in a waves of squeaky *"choo-choos"* it caused his cauldron to be permanently glued to the top of a rock which, by the way, appeared out of thin air.

He wondered for a moment in panic, just how exactly could that have happened. He thought hard and the only reasonable explanation was the sneeze activating a surprise spell. With all he had in himself, he tried to remember the exact sounds the sneeze came with. It was a *"hat-choo-choo"* he was certain for a moment. Then he wondered if it could have been a *"haa-a-cho-choo"* instead. He felt his heart sink.

This was no good, there was no way he could attempt to undo this mysterious matter without knowing what exact spell it was. After a discontented groan, he decided that he had no choice but to think about it some more.

Rain soon filled it up and exotic and local birds stopped by to quench their thirst. When he saw them, the wizard thought that perhaps it was not such a terrible incident after all.

However, it may not always end so well. So solving the problem of not knowing if the wind is quietly lurking around was indeed pressing, because the invisible wind was not something you can direct magic at and exclaim, "Show yourself!" at a time it is quietly waiting to ambush.

Barring it from your land is an impossible task too; it can come and go as it pleases. The wizard had a weather vane in his garden, and it worked well in showing what way the wind was blowing. But this past week, the opponent turned sly and started to rotate it so that it stops at the very exact angle it sat before it was moved. That is why on Monday, Wednesday and Friday the wind played tricks on him, even though the weather vane looked untouched and the wizard assumed the wind was playing elsewhere.

Because, after all, the wind did this to everyone. It was just what the wind does. What else would it do but blow? And when it wasn't blowing his glasses off on purpose, or making him sneeze or close his eyes, it was somewhere else, doing these very same things to someone else. It was an irritating matter and to unwind, the wizard sang a song to mock the wind (and secretly he hoped that if it annoyed the unwanted guest, then it would unintentionally reveal itself).

"I, the wind, hereby
tell you what I do and why.

I wreak havoc on any land,
And fill deserts with dunes of sand.
I batter cliffs by the sea and demand,
That all ships go the way I have planned.

I change hairstyles whenever I please,
And scatter wet laundry just to tease.
I blow pollen to make people sneeze,
Often right after they smile and say 'cheese'!

I fly postcards to where no one sees,
I sprinkle petals in garden teas.
I change ocean currents with ease
And undress autumn trees in a breeze.

It is so much fun, by that I swear,
Wouldn't stop it, wouldn't share.
They scorn at me, but I don't care,
My playground is the whole wide air!

He was chanting this as he walked, when a magpie cried out loudly and flew onto the cauldron. The wizard looked at the bird and saw its blue wing that suddenly looked purple and then blue again as she drank from the cauldron. "What fancy coat this bird has!" thought the wizard and he was suddenly desperate for a change in his own wardrobe.

The magpie was now happily hopping on the grass with a beautiful green hue on its tail. In a momentary ray of sunshine, a wonderful purple sheen appeared on her blue wing, which gave the wizard a grand idea. He rushed back into his house and put a big colander on the table. It could have been a great substitution for a cauldron, if only its use wasn't limited to dry magic. When he needed to stir potions, he had to use a pan.

He took his coat off, but it didn't fit the colander very well. So he untied his hat to use instead. He stopped to look around and checked that the door and windows were closed, as the last thing he wanted to do was to invite the wind in. But naturally, fitting through all cracks and gaps, the wind was already there too, silently waiting.

The house inside was a lot brighter than it seemed from the outside. This was largely because under the floral and leafy blanket, the roof was transparent and the rays of light and shadows of foliage filled the hut with a wild feel. His hut extended underground, and right under the roof he had a tiny and airy upper gallery space where he could sleep and stargaze.

He only had two round windows, one in the front and one it the back. Both of them were covered with red socks hung in rows, to block out unwanted peeks. This also helped the wizard to take a sneaky look at the wind in secret, for it was much easier to move one little piece of the patchwork of socks than to risk moving an entire curtain. Confirming that all were in good order, the wizard put his hand above the colander and with a dusting of magic powder he said,

"The fussy weather can change so sudden,
Clouds come fast and the sun is hidden,

In times of grey clouds and cold, nasty rain,

blue is the colour, the hat should attain!

Once the rain stops and yet the clouds stay,
Green over blue ought to be given way.

When thunder strikes and lightnings echo,
Find your look change to golden yellow.

But should ray of sunshine fall upon you,
Purple shall be your new perfect hue—"

Then he stopped for a second. And the second quickly turned into a minute, as the wizard's face stiffened with trouble. He was about to say what colour the hat should be in windy weather, when he realised something. The weather can be both sunny and breezy. Or rainy and windy. Oh how silly of him not to have thought this through! What would happen then? Would the hat be a mix of colours? Could this make the magic go terribly wrong?

Confused and worried, the wizard was now scared to finish this spell. But the magic dust had already cast a velvety glow on the room, so there was no turning back. Not having any better idea, he thought he would leave it up to magic itself and a bit of luck. So he finished his spell adding,

"And whatever turn the weather may like,
I know there's a colour, perfect to describe,

But which one to pick? I'm not always sure,
For sake of wonder, Magic, please ensure,

That perfect matchings are made for the rest,
I trust your judgement to be the best!"

The magic dust lit the hat up with a pop, and spots of light escaped through the holes on the colander to chase each other on the tabletop.

A moment later the hat started to display a beautiful deep shade of forest green and the magic light went out. Then something else happened. There was a little draught. It was the wind, losing its composure after the exciting magic.

"You sneak!" exclaimed the wizard. "You were here all along!" he added angrily. Then he looked at the hat anxiously. With the little draught the wind caused, the strings of the hat turned crimson red, while the rest of it stayed forest green. A thrill-filled smile appeared on the relieved wizard's face as he uttered happily,

"Lucky, lucky me!
This was meant to be!

Nippy or warm, it does not matter,
Just a mild breeze, or stormy weather,

You are here and the hat knows,
It changes colour when the wind blows.

Your lurking days are practically done,
It's you now this hat keeps an eye on.

Wind and rain are not the same,
Both at the same time is your game.

You see, the weather changes the hat,
But that's not all, be dry or wet,

The string doesn't change, as it knows,
not to turn red, until you are close!"

But the wind was not impressed. Or surprised. And not at all worried. In fact, it looked at the wizard curiously, then chuckled again with a short blow.

"Silly wizard, don't you know,
Just one sudden burst of blow,
And I take the hat and off we go,
We will fly fast, high and low.

Now that it is not on your head,
matters not, if it's green or red,
my biggest worry is, instead,
the hat won't fit the cracks I dread.

I'll find a way out no matter what,

If doors are closed and windows shut,

I'll blow my way out of this hut.

Should windows break, I care not!

The wizard had no time to think through what he heard if he understood the wind at all. The wind was already taking a deep, voluminous breath, and let it all out with a brief, bellowing "shoo" at the back window; which stood no chance against the concentrated blow, giving way almost instantly to the immense force with a loud pop. Red socks flew out scattering all over the green grass and the hat was gliding smoothly in the air, away with the wind. The wizard thought it scandalous. Not his hat! His beloved hat!

"Thief! Stop!" the wizard cried out in anger. "You can't even wear hats!"

"I don't need to wear it, surfing it on pretend waves is fun enough," the wind replied.

"You do speak!" gasped the wizard feebly.

"I blow a lot, I whisper at times and occasionally I speak, yes."

"Then you tell me what your problem is!" the wizard said, recovering from his surprise. "This frolic of yours must stop!"

"You started it!" retorted the wind.

"Me? How?" the wizard was taken aback once again.

"You spoilt my fun, so I take this hat to Northenmost to see what snow does to it."

"Madness!" cried the wizard. "How could I spoil your fun?"

"You stopped me from blowing something," the wind replied. "And you know well, what."

"As if! What could you possibly not blow? You take roofs off if you want to!" the wizard argued.

"I am not really meant to blow roofs off," said the wind bluntly. "I'm not a tornado. But flags are different, and yours are horrible. They made me so sore!"

Sore? The wind? It didn't make sense. In fact, the idea was so bizarre it clogged the wizard's brain tunnels and failed to process. And what flags? He saw little merit in trying to argue, but for the sake of his hat, he tried his chances nevertheless.

"But I have not got any flags," he said, hoping the wind would elaborate.

"Sure you do! A week ago you put some on your door. But it's all just tricks and deception! They are firmly affixed! Not even a loose thread to move!" the wind raged. "I must blow flags to make them dance. You should know that. But these ones don't! I tried blowing stronger, and stronger but nothing! I had to give up, which made me feel not only silly and embarrassed, but rather sore as well! You would have no idea how hard I tried, it was exhausting! I even brought over some really heavy clouds."

The wizard thought of the heavy rain last week as he looked at his door. It was shut, displaying the little plates, forks, spoons and napkins stuck on it.

"The napkins," he muttered in awe. "Those are napkins, not flags!"

"Liar!" roared the wind. The leaves that were lying on the ground peacefully were suddenly thrown in the air with anger and twirled fast before being tossed back down with force.

"But honestly, they are not meant to be there," insisted the wizard.

"Then how come they are? They weren't always there!"

"I know how they became stuck, but it was not intentional," he explained and then sighed.

"But, aren't you a wizard? It should be easy for you to fix it," the wind said, sounding important. "Do it now!"

"Don't you think I tried? I can't."

"Why?"

"I'm bad at… magic," the wizard muttered reluctantly under his breath.

"How come?" asked the wind.

"I don't know," he said. " Things I do often go wrong. Like the dinnerware glued to the front door. They were meant to be flown back into the kitchen cabinet."

"Really? " asked the wind surprised.

"Yes," said the wizard curtly. He looked rather sad now.

"Are you trying to trick me again?" the wind still sounded dubious.

"No!" huffed the wizard and looked away, crossing his arms in a hostile manner. "Like I said, I didn't mean to deceive you with the napkins either."

A sudden burst of air ran around the wizard, tickling his nose and chin which made him crack a short laugh.

"Oh, please don't tickle me!" he pleaded.

"Can't you just be something else then?" asked the wind as it stopped tickling.

"You mean like a bus driver who accidentally turns the bus into a flying tortoise and lands its passengers on a faraway galaxy, if I ever manage to make it stop at all? Because if I don't then maybe it will just go until our hair is so long that it will be caught on a random star," the wizard gabbled.

"A mighty fine adventure I say, just right for a wizard, indeed. Now that I think about it, I couldn't be anything else either," said the wind, but the kind words failed to console the wizard, who kept staring at an autumn leaf on the ground with a face too glum.

"Does messing up sometimes make you bad at something?" asked the wind curiously.

"I think so," replied the wizard.

Terrible silence spread around as the leaves suddenly fell from the air like heavy objects. Then came a sharp whistle as the wind wailed with despair, "Oh no! Then I am not good at being the wind either! In fact, I must be terrible!"

"I don't think it's possible for you to be bad at being the wind," the wizard said hastily to calm the wind.

"But I often do things I don't mean to," said the wind but didn't continue.

"Such as?" asked the wizard, seriously wondering.

"The other day, I had to, I absolutely had to move some air about near the riverside. After lots of heavy rain, the fastest way to dry it all up is to sweep through with very strong blows. So you see it was indeed much needed. But then... I caught a boy's glasses."

The wizard recalled his own experience of windsurfing glasses. He felt for the boy already.

"They landed on the edge of the pavement, and the boy yelled out. I stopped to look, but it was too late. A delayed gust pushed them right into the river; they were out of sight within seconds. I did want to, but you see, no matter how hard I tried I just could not blow them back on the boy's face. I thought I should be able to do it, after all it was me who blew them off, right? But for some reason I just couldn't. So I am probably not very good at what I am doing either," finished the wind.

The wizard fell silent. The wind's problem now seemed as real as his own.

"Maybe some things are meant to be, even if they don't feel right, so we can learn from them," the wizard said. "Not including my glasses which were *not* meant to be blown off on purpose!"

"That's right, I'm sorry. But to make up for the tease, I have good news for you," the wind replied. The wizard's eyes grew big showing glossy curiosity. He was going to keep his hat!

"I kept an eye on the frog you enchanted. Within a few

days it shrank back to its original size. So you shouldn't worry about finding it any more." Despite not meeting his expectation, a delighted smile still brightened the wizard's face up.

"Really? That's lovely news indeed!" he rejoiced. "But wait, that means my spell wasn't permanent! Do you think my cauldron shall hover again? Might that dinnerware also find a way back to my kitchen cabinet?" the wizard kept asking with excitement.

"Perhaps. You can only wait and see," replied the wind. "Though I suspect that if your plates let go they will break."

"You can try catching them with the napkins," smiled the wizard. "If you are strong and fast enough."

"I do like a challenge!"

"Shall I also tell you something? To make up for thinking you only do mean things."

The wind nodded. Or at least, the wizard had a feeling that it did. "You shouldn't feel silly and embarrassed. No one can see you, you are invisible!" he said with a chuckle then he burst into laughter as the wind gave him a good tickle in return.

"You know, I thought so hard this week to find a way to predict your presence. All I should have done was set up a flag that you cannot help but blow," concluded the wizard, still laughing. "Oh, how wrong I was!"

"We both did our best at being wrong for long enough," the wind added. "We should try the opposite from now on." The wizard wondered whether that meant doing their worst at being wrong or doing their best at being right, but then he realised, that they both meant the same. And that's just what they did.

And all was good on Planet Best At,
And we should go and leave it at that.

But, there's just one more thing,
To your attention I must bring,
And no, that isn't the new flag that
the wind could now happily blow at.

But that it didn't all end with luck,
That poor little frog was stuck,
With a tongue all normal in daylight,
But one that would glow every night.
Of this no one ever knew,
Except, of course, now you.

The Chauns

I looked at him and said, "the end,
I hope now you'll be my friend."
But he stood there, silent and still;
a tear in his eye starting to spill.

"Oh dear, no!" I cried, "the frog's fine!
I swear he is well, dandy, divine!
I meant no harm, please don't be sad,
Or was the story truly that bad?"

"The story was fine," he kindly said,
"it was your wizard's mix-up that led
me to think of a friend I've got,
who also gets things wrong a lot.

But now I'm lost, I might never see him,
or the others, as I've been so dim."
At once I said, "I'll help you out!"
With joy he jumped and started to shout,

"It's that way I'm sure, or there, or there!"
I looked, but he pointed everywhere.
I said, "We'll choose one path to walk,
And I'll learn of your home whilst we talk.

Come sit closer to my ear,
So your stories I can hear,
Should we head the wrong way,
I'll change route with no delay."

He climbed up fast with his tiny frame
and told me Connie was his name.
Cosy on my woolly neckwear,
his adventures he began to share.

It didn't take long for me to see,
Everything he described to me.
In my mind it all looked so real,
Even their bond I could strangely feel.

They were all tiny like him,
But not all of them quite so slim.
A type of unknown leprechauns,
Simply calling themselves "*Chauns*".

Chauns climb fast, strong and steady,
To dart ahead they are always ready.
Almost all textures they can conquer,
but if there's gloss they must surrender.

In their own unique way,
They hear more than words can say.
Hence they talk to bees and the birds,
In a world that needs no words.

These fellas are fine without food,
But should they see something good,
Chances are they'll have a bite,
Which, like their weight, is quite light.

Two of them make lovely attire,
The kind that anyone would admire,
Another planned games to play,
they never had a boring day.

He spoke fast, his stories were long,
And here or there contained a song.
I let him talk, took notes in my head,
And later wrote down all the things he said.

These are the stories he told en route,
And their trueness no one can refute.
Many will try regardless, I'm sure,
But those doubters, no doctor can cure.

Ignore them, they just don't know,
That this tale began long ago.
A time forgotten but not gone,
And still today it carries on.

I hope you will now see it too,
Their life, as you read through,
Whether their world is a wonderful kind,
You can make up your own mind.

Marcherries

Connie opened his eyes and found himself in a dark and tight capsule. He had an awful night and ended up tossing and turning until he became the stuffing in his blanket roll. When he finally managed to unwrap himself he looked for the others, but he was alone on the frame.

They had left without waking Connie because they knew that the only thing worse than waking Connie up on purpose was to do it accidentally and then having to try to find a poor Chaun to take the blame. They all slept on this very picture frame—a nice golden colour and matt surface—only Tuff and Ninian had separate bunks. Ninian hated noise and company so he found himself a distant spot, and Tuff slept on the highest part of the frame; the top of the lamp placed above it. Tuff was the strongest and his warm spot had to be won but so far none of them had managed to arm-wrestle him for it. Connie looked up, but he sensed no presence from there either.

He only wore a pair of dusty-blue trousers held up by crossed suspenders and his small grey figure moved obscurely as he made his way to the edge to look around.

He inspected the room keenly, furrowing his eyebrows below his arched forehead, and his eyes moved fast in contrast to the still dark dot under his left eye. The room was quiet and tranquil but as he listened very carefully, he picked up a faint voice from the opposite wall.

With their exceptional senses, Chauns could hear and locate each other's voice from as far away as a room and a half, and as long as they were not hiding they could easily spot each other from a good distance, too. They were most likely under the right-hand black and gold built-in veneered cabinet, which stood beneath a tall gilded mirror and was one of four identical pieces, each placed near a corner, facing each other in pairs. This was their usual assembly point so Connie felt the morning was off to a regular start.

He grabbed his soft, velvety blanket with both hands and held it up as a parachute as he leapt from the frame. The yellow flower petal glided smoothly in the air, falling and gradually lowering the teeny Chaun. Just before he hit the thick rug he let go and landed softly into a crouch, grabbed his petal nearing him from above, and with it secured on his back by his braces, he ran to the others.

On the vast open floor he sped up significantly,

something they all could do when they were running in an unbroken line, saving them a lot of time when trekking through the large rooms. He found six Chauns there with Yeo—the game rep—standing in the centre, a brown peppercorn at his feet. He looked like Connie, same height and round head, but his forehead was taller with a headband going around it; tied on the left side, the loose straps dangled down behind his pointy ear, past his shoulders. He wore a light vest tucked into his shorts.

"Hey guys, what are you doing?" Connie asked Tuff, who stood closest to him. Tuff was Connie's height but he wore longer trousers, his arms were strong and bulky and his eyes narrow and authoritative. He also had a good chunk of his left ear missing which gave him a tough look.

"Yeo is still trying to figure out the rules to this game he saw them watch," answered Tuff and he lightly kicked the peppercorn away from Yeo's feet towards Elma and Anglo. Anglo was the tallest of them all and his ears were pointing higher up. His trousers were high waisted and long.

In contrast, Elma was the smallest and thinnest. Her petite figure was made to seem even more fragile by the tight clothes she wore and the small round bun on top of her head, which highlighted her curvy, elegant ears. Elma's face brightened up as the dry orb approached her with its random, bumpy roll. She tried to pass it on but Yeo stood in its way.

"No play until we are clear on all of the rules," he said with great importance.

"Come on, this is boring, let's just play!" said Tuff vehemently to Yeo, but Yeo was having none of it. He picked up the peppercorn and held it tight.

"There are two teams, two goals, a ball and a boss. The boss tells the other players when to fall, when to kick each other and when to kick the ball, how to run and in what direction to score. It's all up to the boss—" Yeo carried on with the textbook.

"That doesn't sound right," said Anglo and Elma at the same time.

"Or fun," added Loch, who had a tall forehead and only one strap crossing his upper body to hold up his loose trousers, which were gathered at the knees.

"Oh but it is, you'll see. The *ginormees* were absolutely glued to their screen when they were watching this game. Like I said, the boss rules and when the players don't listen to the boss they receive cards. Now I just need to figure out what happens when the ball goes beyond the lines..." murmured Yeo scratching his head and looking at imaginary borders on the floor. "I wish I had seen more than a minute of it...."

"Who'll be the boss?" asked Anglo jokingly.

"Another game will decide that," began Yeo, but Stoop and Stump — whom everyone called the Duo, for they were identical — cut him off. They looked exactly like Connie, but with a spiky top of a head each and no dots under their left eyes.

"Nay, nay," they chimed leaning against the skirting, yawning.

"That again?" barked Yeo. "No way? Quit being lazy and talk so that others can understand!"

"UERNUDLANG!" replied Stump and threw an ugly grimace at Yeo.

"I can neither earn nor learn your pointless noodle language!" snapped Yeo back at them but their ominous silence and impassive face indicated that the Duo have reached their morning input words-wise.

Soon they were all smiles again though, for the ball was in motion and fun began when Anglo distracted Yeo, and Loch hit the hollow globe out of his hands. Off they ran with it, before Yeo registered the events.

"That's it then," yelled Yeo, "I'm the boss! And that's a red card! Make it two actually! Stop I say, stop!" He ran after the others, but fell behind terribly.

"Score!" cried Loch after Anglo hit a Chaun-foot sized chip on the cabinet leg with the peppercorn.

"Pre—," began Yeo but he was cut off again.

"P...ostros!" laughed Anglo and passed the ball to the Duo.

"No!" cried Yeo. "It's...it's pre-po-sterous! Preposterous!" He had to stop to catch his breath after shouting and running at the same time but successfully added, "Obey the rules!"

"Rules? You mean something like the boss taking the blame when they come looking for the peppercorn-thief?" beamed Anglo at him.

"Oh no!" Elma said and drew away from the game. "Did we steal this?"

"No, I promise I found it lying here yesterday," Yeo confirmed, but Elma was hopelessly worried and withdrew from the party to look for Hetty and Hammy, who were away foraging. The Duo, Anglo and Loch kept on playing so Tuff, who until now just stood by chatting to Connie, also joined in. Yeo put a strong —but blatantly destroyed—face on and tried his best at being boss again, but was obviously hurt and sulky about his pepper game going pear-shaped.

Connie watched them, counting all the Chauns present when a distant voice called his name. He spun around, scanning the room for Lillian and soon found her small figure standing at the bottom of the nearest door frame.

"Connie, come there's a window open in the Music Room," she said whilst waving at him excitedly. Connie waved back giving a shout to the group that he and Lillian were to go outside, then ran to join her. Lillian had a tall forehead with slightly pointed arches, curly ears, and wore a sleeveless dotty dress. Emerging from the top of her head, two loose ponytails framed her face; each with curled, bouncy ends nudging her waist.

The Music Room, too, was devoid of human presence so they ran freely on the parquet flooring, their favourite surface, which provided the best grip and smoothness, always resulting in a marvellous sprint.

It was a nippy but bright morning and when they reached the outer windowsill and the decorative balcony mounted in front of it, Connie and Lillian climbed into a large gap to look down at the long and wide terrace below. The bordering lower stone fence—broken in the middle for grand, solid steps—outlined the way to the garden paths and the lawn. He reached for his petal and so did Lillian, as they readied themselves to descend. Then Connie had a thought.

"Whoever lands first wins," he said.

"Wins what?"

"A petal," Connie answered. "Yesterday, I saw them carrying a pot of mini roses in the gallery. I'm hoping they didn't take it very far."

"Mini roses! They are so cosy," Lillian said with glistening eyes. "My petal is battered, so one of those would be so lush tonight!"

"Now, now, no blaming the tatty petal for losing the race," Connie said.

"I wasn't trying to do so," Lillian answered defensively. "I only said it so you don't feel at a disadvantage." She glanced at Connie's petal; it was hopelessly bruised everywhere.

"Don't worry I'll put up an honest fight for it," Connie said with a smile. "But you'd love it too I'm sure, I only saw it for a second but it was so beautiful, I've never seen one like it before."

"I bet it smells wonderful," said Lillian thinking of the lovely and delicate traces of scents they could pick up from petals, even if it was too faint for other noses to note.

"But wait, why not go and search for it together?" Lillian asked. "We could each have one."

"Well, it's perfectly possible that we shall both land at the very same time!"

"Go on then!" Lillian said with a big smile. She knew that Connie was always after an adventure or two.

They counted to three then began to lower themselves at the mercy of the petal. Connie was ahead of Lillian heading towards the grass, but Lillian's petal took her to the elevated banister of the stone steps, which meant that she landed first.

"I guess this counts as a fair win," Connie said once he emerged from the thick grass. "I'll search for it later for you. But this grass needs cutting so I think they'll come today to sort it. It's best if we head towards the trees. Let's leave our petals, they have seen better days."

Lillian nodded and they began walking to the right where the winding footpaths lead. They rarely crossed the whole length of the lawn because of the big lake on the other side, but they did like to roam around in it when they felt like jungle-trekking or looking around.

The view from the middle of the lawn, whilst stood

on top of a sturdy blade of grass, showed the whole estate which they were very fond of. The nearby walls— of none other than Buckingham Palace—looked huge, grand and daunting to the Chauns, who were just tiny flecks in comparison. The sight fascinated them and the thought of secretly living in it was both exciting and timorous.

Mystery surrounds how they came to be there, however. Connie said they had once fallen into something with such smooth and glossy sides that they couldn't climb out. Instead, the Dark Float came, by which they meant the deepest darkness pouring in only to linger. At first they panicked, filling the darkness with screams and fruitless attempts to escape, but it was no use. Once they calmed down it didn't take long for boredom to join the party under the dark hood.

They boycotted them both by taking a long nap, hoping they would see light when they woke. This wish of theirs sort of came true, but it gave them the scare of their life, for they woke to a sudden sharp noise and light everywhere.

The Dark Float and glossy surfaces were gone and they had no idea what was happening or where they were. Amidst the commotion in the room—about some broken china—they ran for cover under the nearest cabinet, and then their eyes instantly locked in on the perfect place for a more permanent shelter.

It was truly inviting. A gorgeous, tall painting bordered by a wide and embellished golden frame, with a path to it that felt specifically tailor-made for Chauns, so as soon as they were left alone they made a dash for it. They crossed the rug in a straight line with increasing speed that powered a long jump onto one end of the gilded and heavily decorated fireguard.

It led them to the upper part of the stone fireplace, a cold but velvety white stone that they climbed easily to reach the top, where three short and curvy vases and two tall candle holders adorned the mantelpiece. It was one of the latter they used to reach the luscious goal—the gilded and swirly picture frame leading up so high that their only objective became to conquer it the moment they saw it. On the top of it, at just the right height, they would have the chance to think in peace and find answers.

For that they climbed the matt and mildly rough golden surface eagerly, but comprehension of their situation and whereabouts did not meet them there. There was only one thing they were certain of—they very much liked it here. This room was magnificent everywhere they looked. The tall windows letting endless light in to reflect off the mirrors not only filled the room with brightness, but added sparkles to the dominantly gold features of the room.

Having nowhere else in mind to call home, they set one up right here. Soon they became accustomed to the errands that took place and stopped questioning the mysterious times before the Dark Float, especially since it made their heads feel fuzzy.

As they became more familiar with the estate, they grew fond of exploring the palace and the gardens. They avoided certain areas because of the heavy presence of people, but overall they wandered around carefree, mostly on this floor.

Now, too, Connie and Lillian were running ahead at ease on the footpaths.

"I can see Rusty!" shouted Connie pointing at a robin on the grass nearby. She was the only bird they were friends with, and she let them climb on her back today as well. Rusty was always kind and took them far into the gardens where the trees were taller with thicker crowns, which made the journey quicker, because Rusty could fly faster than the top speed the Chauns could ever achieve.

Connie and Lillian really liked the forest. For them, even this smaller group of garden trees was a huge green labyrinth—perfect for adventure. After walking around a little, Connie stopped to look at the bright, blue sky, but his eyes caught something nearer instead. He pointed upward and said with excitement, "Lillian, look! What could that be?"

Lillian looked up but couldn't see what Connie was pointing at. "What am I to look at?" she asked.

"That red shine up high! Look! Right there, on a branch," he rushed to say. "Do you think it could be cherries?" he added impatiently.

Lillian kept looking and saw a faint red shine up high, when the clouds let the sun reach it briefly.

"How could they be? It's only March, Connie!" she said doubtingly. Connie looked at Lillian with a passive frown.

"Really, Lillian, so what! Nobody at the palace knows of our existence. There could be plenty out there we might not know about, like wonder Marcherries!" he said and his mouth curled up at the thought of the juicy red fruit.

And he was already jumping on the roots of the tree,

ready to climb up on it. Lillian sighed, she had little confidence about the goal, but followed him so as not to be left behind. The cracked bark coating the tree, forming zigzag tunnels, did not resemble a cherry tree but did make the way up easier. When they reached the branch they needed, they walked on it to the red things. As they came closer to it, they saw that it was only one thing, not round or big enough to be a cherry. It was far too sparkly and vivid as well, with a stiff golden stalk. Connie touched it—it was hard and cold.

"What is it?" asked Lillian.

"I'm not sure but I have a feeling I have seen it before," replied Connie. "I just haven't a clue where. Maybe it was a very long time ago, a time we are not meant to remember."

"No, I also think I have seen it before," Lillian added. "Maybe we need to try not remembering and it will come to us."

"That never worked regarding the Dark Float," Connie reminded her, but they left it at that and climbed up a bit higher.

"What a wonderful view," commented Lillian. Indeed, some shorter evergreen trees were sprinkled with shiny highlights by the sun and as they moved in the breeze, they formed long, radiant waves among the bare ones.

They curled up in a bark ridge and heard the gardeners begin to cut the grass. The buzzing noise of the lawnmowers and the soft breeze made the Chauns doze off; when they woke the sun was straight above the trees and they heard the lawnmowers stop.

"We must go Lillian," said Connie. "We've been here far too long!"

"Are we going to leave that here?" Lillian pointed down at the sparkly object hanging from the branch beneath. They still didn't know what exactly it was. Connie thought for a moment.

"It's big and looks heavy," he said and shrugged. "I think we've got no choice but to leave it. It's no use to us."

Connie headed to the trunk but Lillian didn't follow him, for she just realised something.

"Don't worry, we won't fall from this tree," Connie said without turning around

"I wish we had the petals still. Oh, why did I agree to come up?" Lillian said feebly, the tree seemed to be a lot higher than their bunk.

"Don't worry, we'll sing the lemon song and it'll be

fun," he smiled and looked at her. Lillian's face lit up a bit and Connie began the chime:

> "There are no sweet lemons out there Sir,
> As if there were,
> Something else would have to be bitter.
>
> If that something's also yellow, round,
> And can be found,
> Up the trees high, far from the ground,
>
> They'll look the same, some bitter some sweet,
> Oh what a treat,
> Not knowing which one to choose to eat.
>
> But this problem is in fact rather small,
> Because after all,
> We know for sure, no doubt, as I recall,
>
> That,
>
> There are no sweet lemons out there sir,
> As if there were..."

They sang together, repeating it again and again until they safely reached the ground where they stopped to catch their breath.

"See, all good!" Connie said and they headed towards the open lawn, where they saw the chief gardener loading her ride-on lawn mower so they made a good run for it and they sped up as they dashed through the dense grassland, manoeuvring incredibly well among the stalks. When they reached her they jumped on, and just in time as well, for she drove off towards the palace. Thanks to their lucky ride, they were just below the terrace when they jumped off.

"You climb up Lillian," Connie said. "I'll go in downstairs."

"Are you sure we shouldn't both go?" Lillian asked with concern. "We tend to avoid the downstairs area."

"Yes, it'll be fine. I won't be long," Connie said. "But you better go and let the others know where I went."

"OK, but don't worry if you can't do it, we are never short of flowers here. So much so that all of us can have a different coloured one all the time," said Lillian, and with that Connie ran off.

When Lillian reached the Music Room she saw people standing beside the doors like guards. However, their bodies and eyes were as motionless as the clouds in some of the landscape paintings, so she entered with confidence and ran across the floor without having to be careful.

When she crossed into the White Drawing Room she heard Chaun voices from their usual assembly point so she headed that way. When she reached them, Anglo, Elma, Tuff and Loch were all talking fast and at the same time. Something had happened, that much was obvious and now Lillian wished Connie hadn't gone off alone.

The Duo were quiet at the skirting and Yeo was furthest away sulking in the corner, but at least he had the peppercorn. Lillian clapped once to call their attention and asked what the disturbance was about.

"Some jewels went missing!" cried Elma looking worried and anxious.

"It was an earring," explained Tuff.

"Why is that a problem for us?" asked Lillian looking confused with the news. Palace matters hardly ever interfered with their lives.

"Think about it! If they can't locate it soon they will have to go search for it. They will come and look at everything, absolutely everywhere, and when they come and look close enough, they might end up seeing us!" cried Elma. "Maybe they will even use a magnifying glass!" she muttered slowly with a petrified face.

"Not a magnifying glass! That would be really bad," added Loch shaking off a quick shiver.

Lillian thought it through and it was a possibility, indeed.

"And when they find it they will come for the peppercorn next," Anglo said teasingly to which Elma's complexion faded as her face turned sour with worry.

"How did it go missing?" Lillian asked, shooting a warning frown at Anglo.

"A maid was polishing them upstairs and held one up and out against the sun to see how it lights up the ruby. But when someone knocked on the door she jumped and let go of the earring, tossing it through the open window," Elma explained.

"Or at least, that's what she says," Loch added.

"So we know where it is?" Lillian asked with relief.

"No, she went down to find it but it was nowhere. The poor girl is in absolute tears. No one believes her," Anglo said. "So they are going to search the palace to make sure it hasn't been taken or hidden."

Lillian nodded absent-mindedly whilst wondering what Connie would do. He would not stand still and rattle like a leaf in fear but go with Tuff to stop the danger.

"We must find it now and bring it back then," she said confidently. "So what is it that we are looking for?"

"It's a ruby earring. You can see it on that portrait, look," said Tuff whilst pointing at a painting on the wall. It featured a pair of red earrings dangling from an elegant lady's ears.

"Hetty really likes that painting. I wonder where they are, and also where's—" Tuff began.

"I know where this is!" cried Lillian. "But it's not on the ground. Connie's wonder-cherry looked exactly like these!"

The others gave her a very funny look, so Lillian hurriedly explained how they climbed up a tree thinking that something red and shiny could be cherries.

Lillian stared at the painting. "He was right, we must've seen them before."

"This is ridiculous," said Loch. "You have no chance of bringing this back. You wouldn't be able to move it, like ever."

"You cannot know that for sure," Lillian argued.

"I can doubt it with good heart and clear conscience," Loch finished the debate.

"Leave her, Loch," Tuff said. "Where's Connie?"

"I don't think he will be back for a while. He went to find the mini roses they have somewhere because he owes me a petal."

"Mini roses!" cried Elma, forgetting all about the dangers worrying her a minute ago. She looked mesmerised with the thought of them and her face was truly alive again.

"Lillian, where is this tree?" asked Tuff.

"It's out in the garden," she replied. "Sadly, not very close."

Tuff said nothing, and for a minute they were all deep in thoughts. Except Elma, who was trotting around like a peacock, still thinking of the rose.

"Let's ask Rusty to help," Lillian said, hoping that Rusty would actually be around. "But I will need you to come with me," she added looking at Tuff.

"Don't tell me it looked heavy," Loch blurted out.

"I didn't and I won't," Lillian said with a confident smile.

Tuff walked to a crack in the skirting and fished out two petals from their secret hiding place, which they used for storing blankets during the day and other objects they used, and gave one to Lillian.

"Yeo, you stay here because I know you hurt yourself during the kick-about. The others should go and find Connie and return to the bunk for cover," he said sternly not giving Yeo a chance to act tough and hide his pain.

"Wish us luck!" Lillian said and ran off back towards the Music Room with Tuff.

After they had left, Yeo—still holding the peppercorn —came forward with a slight limp and said they shouldn't all go and look for Connie because it would be too chaotic, not to mention Hetty and Hammy might come back. He suggested Anglo should definitely go though, because he was the tallest and the best climber; but Anglo was lazy and not going was a definite option so he said, "forget it." The Duo, however, happily volunteered.

"Weo, weo!" they jumped around.

"Absolutely not," said Yeo and raised his palm to protest. "Nobody needs your encrypted information. It'd be faster to chew myself through walls *and* paintings to see what's up than to crack your code."

"They'd definitely come search for us if you chewed holes in their paintings," Anglo joked.

"I'll go with them and then there are no issues," said Elma.

"You'd just panic about everything!" Loch said. "I'll go with Anglo, the two of us will be enough to watch out for as well as Connie."

Anglo raised his eyebrows and kept them there masterfully whilst staring at Loch disapprovingly.

"You are coming, end of, " Loch said. "Or I'll weave spider web all around your head whilst you sleep!" Anglo's eyebrows stayed in place but his mouth drooped significantly.

"No! That's so disgusting, it's light and long and so hard to get rid of, it clings to you like mud except this you can't wash off and makes you paranoid for days even when it's gone! Don't, please don't do that it's just so gross, so yuck—so *fooy!*" Anglo wailed and was now willing to go conquer the whole palace, each and every floor of it.

"Un! Un!" the Duo jumped around Yeo, laughing and nudging the ball out from his hands after Loch and Anglo left.

"I should have made you two go after all. . . . " sighed Yeo with a heavy face and hobbled back to the skirting to sit down.

By now Lillian and Tuff had raced through masses of the freshly cut grass looking for Rusty, but they couldn't see her. Tuff suggested that they head towards the trees on foot, even if it takes longer, the most time they can waste is to wait in vain, when something big approaching from the sky distracted him.

"Look, Lillian! A crow!" he said whilst pointing at it. "It's looking to land!"

Lillian crouched behind a wide and thick cut blade of grass. "We can't just run up to crows! They would try to eat us, or worse still—tread on us!" she yelled.

"We will hop on before they have a chance to do so," Tuff replied calmly and ran closer to where he guessed the crow was most likely to land. Lillian looked at him with a horrified face, just the mere thought of his suggestion made her want to crawl somewhere deep underground.

"Maybe this very crow took the earring!" Tuff tried to convince Lillian. "Hurry up, we will have to jump at the same time, as it will make him fly away for sure!"

"I think it would be a lot safer to just find another home...." Lillian murmured but ran towards the bird nonetheless, for Tuff was certainly going for it. They hopped onto its bumpy claws together, which felt surprisingly firm with deep ridges that they could grip easily. The crow spread its wings and promptly flew off with the stowaways clinging on firmly.

"I wonder, Tuff, what would happen if it didn't head towards the trees?" asked Lillian with a distressed face. Tuff panicked. He sort of assumed the trees would be the definite destination. Where else would it like to go?

For a few seconds his feet felt numb, but soon relief

filled them with life again as the bird was indeed flying towards the tree crowns. Except, a few moments later it became obvious that landing wasn't an imminent plan.

"We are going to have to let go!" Tuff said boldly. "Unless you want us to land somewhere further away from the earring than we were at the start!"

"When do we let go?" Lillian asked with great concern.

"How am I supposed to know? Which tree was it?" Tuff yelled at her.

"Somewhere in the middle, but I am not that sure," said Lillian and she had no chance to worry about it any more as they were already passing big chunks of the garden trees.

"Make it *now*! Let go!" Tuff bellowed as he dived down, aiming for the leafy tree crowns. "Don't forget to hold up your petal!"

But owing to the circumstances, Lillian was not focusing well and as she tried to grab hold of the petal, it flew out of her hand.

"Nooo! Rusty," she screeched in fear as she fell fast, past Tuff who looked on with horror on his face. "Rusty! Rusty! Come help me, please! Rusty!"

Lillian was still screaming when she landed on a fat, somewhat hairy and soft leaf; it gave her a light bounce until she managed to grab the midrib. Shortly afterwards Tuff, who navigated the petal masterfully, landed not far from her and made his way to her at once.

"Are you all right?" he asked. "I thought you were a goner."

"So did I," Lillian said still slightly in shock. "But luck is on our side today, look!"

Tuff searched the spot she pointed at with his eyes and saw the delightful shine of the earring hanging on a branch close by. Once they reached it however, they discovered another obstacle, and that was being short of hands. They couldn't carry it down when they needed their hands to reach the ground later.

"Why did we not bring Loch, too?" asked Lillian.

"You know what, I'm not really sure," answered Tuff shaking his head lightly. "But it wouldn't have helped if you think about it."

"True, " Lillian said. "Should we just free it and let it fall to the ground?"

"That way we might never find it. Look, it could fall anywhere and be lost among grass or fallen leaves on the ground." They both looked down, thinking of all the places the earring could land and, indeed, the possibilities seemed endless to the tiny Chauns up high.

They were so deep in thought that they hardly noticed the branch they stood on lowering with additional weight. Rusty arrived and her landing set the branch in a slow, sweeping motion. They looked at the robin and their face brightened up with joy.

"Rusty!" cried Lillian. "How come you are here?"

"You called me!" Rusty replied. "It took me some time to find you."

"Oh Rusty! How fantastic! We could seriously do with your help," Lillian rushed to say. "Please, can you fly us back to the palace with this earring?"

Rusty didn't reply, just eyed the earring suspiciously.

"For a piece of walnut maybe?" Lillian tried to convince her and leaned towards the bird with hopeful eyes, knowing that without the petal she would have to climb again. Rusty looked at her pensively but then she nodded and said, "I can try."

"Thanks!" rejoiced Lillian. "It's a promise, though I will need time to plan the walnut mission if that's all right?"

Rusty nodded again and spread her wing. Tuff and Lillian climbed on, looking forward to a much nicer ride back. Then Rusty cleverly lifted the earring away from the branch with her beak and set off towards the palace;

where an awful lot has happened whilst Lillian and Tuff were chasing fake cherries.

Anglo and Loch had found the flowers a few rooms away in the State Dining Room. The flamboyant red and yellow striped roses were beaming. A man was wrapping them in a transparent and shiny sheet, which crackled loudly whilst being gathered and tied tightly on the top, completely enclosing the flowers.

A giant red bow with sparkling edging soon found itself in the wrong place with the wrong task—trying to decorate the stunning roses. Perhaps, based on the overall outcome, it wasn't too sinister for Anglo and Loch to liken the finish to a Chaun repelling barricade.

"That's one way to stop petal-hunting, huh?" asked Loch, but Anglo didn't reply, just kept staring at it in motionless silence.

"You reckon they trapped him in there?" he said eventually.

The thought was chilling and it froze them to the spot, but only momentarily, as the loud voice of the man quickly returned them to a state of readiness.

"This to be delivered to the address provided," he said to a lady who just entered. "Make sure it is received by no other than the addressee and do not let it topple."

She nodded and took the flowers.

"The car is waiting outside and shall bring you back straight away."

"Will the guards search this?" the lady asked raising the flowers slightly.

"No, it's all been taken care of. Regardless of recent events, this must be sent today."

She nodded again and turned around to set off.

"Connie!" Loch yelled really loudly from the bottom of the door frame as her steps approached.

The woman stopped and looked back.

"Did you say something?" she asked but the man shook his head so she carried on.

With every step her shoes awoke a loud, echoing thump repeatedly choked by another and another as she walked. Connie waited for one of these to cry, "help me!"

Loch and Anglo began to run after them, her steps were brisk and long.

"We should let the others know," began Anglo without stopping.

"No time! They are in the other direction," replied Loch. "Unless you spot Hetty, Hammy or Ninian on the way we are all Connie can count on."

But they had no time to look around. So Anglo went bananas and started not too loudly calling out the names of the Chauns who may be nearby. They were in luck because Hetty and Hammy were foraging near the side entrance the lady headed for. When she stopped to speak to a palace guard, Loch and Anglo jumped onto her shoes, which Hetty and Hammy took notice of.

Whilst the guard listened to her errand and beckoned knowingly, they dashed for her shoes too and successfully joined Loch and Anglo. Hammy and Hetty were both short and rather stumpy. Their eyes were friendly and filled with curiosity.

Hetty had ears like Elma and Lillian, pointy forehead arches, curls above her shoulders and a long, wide skirt, whilst Hammy had small pointy ears, a tall curvy forehead and semi-tight shorts.

As they were carried outside, the chauffeur had already been waiting with the car's door open. The lady carefully placed the roses on the passenger seat, intending to hold it through the drive. Rusty, Lillian and Tuff at this moment were circling above the estate, unsure of where to take the earring.

Lillian spotted the four tiny Chauns running to the car wheels and shouted, "Rusty, drop the earring where those people are!" The robin was overjoyed to finally let go of it and dropped the earring to land right behind the lady. The chauffeur took notice of the subtle sound it made and picked it up.

"Madam, I'm afraid you may have dropped this," he held the earring out to her and she looked at it strangely.

They didn't pay attention to the robin that landed on the top of the car or the little Chauns who started climbing up on the tyres, trying to approach the passenger seat.

"It's not mine. But good grief!" she blurted. "Could this be the one they are missing?"

She took the earring and started walking back to the palace saying, "I'll be right back!"

"No problem madam," the chauffeur replied and took a cloth out of his pocket to buff the car, during which he closed the door. By this time the little Chauns were inside.

"Oh no! We are trapped!" Hetty cried as the door closed with a bang.

"And we haven't even rescued Connie yet!" Hammy added to the woes. "Connie, hang in there!"

Connie's little head appeared at the brim of the pot, a hopeful grin on his face.

"We will be taken somewhere far away! Maybe we will be locked in the dark again!" panicked Hetty.

"Stop that talk and free Connie!" said Loch. "When she comes back the door will be opened again. We all need to be ready to leave then!"

The little Chauns looked at the wrapped roses.

"I'm not going near that," said Hammy discovering something more grave than being trapped.

"Me either," agreed Hetty solemnly.

"Let me guess," began Loch, "It's too ugly?"

"Yes, but no, it's not that. It's glitter. If it falls on me I'll look reflective and highly visible," explained Hammy.

"It sticks to you like—" began Hetty but Anglo finished it for her.

"Cob web," he said with disgust.

"Worse, actually," Hammy corrected him and Anglo tried to shake off the thought.

"Would it interfere with our protection charm?" Loch asked.

"Makes me wonder. I have no idea," replied Hammy.

"Forget the glitter, what are we to do with this transparent cover?" asked Anglo.

"We can't climb it by the look of it," began Loch,

"we'll have to pierce it with something sharp."

Hetty was always ready for moments to create things. This one gave her an opportunity to create a much needed doorway, so from her pocket she produced the smallest wooden needle ever heard of. They ran to the base of the pot and she pierced the foil, pulling the needle up and down to make way for Connie. To help her, Hammy and Loch pulled the squeaky sheet to the sides. Thirsty for air, the clear wrap burst open hastily, and the Chauns quickly let go.

"Oh no," said Hetty. "It ripped too much!"

"Don't worry, they won't notice," Hammy said. "And even if they do, we will be long gone!"

"Hopefully," commented Loch warily.

"Connie, come down quick!" said Hammy, waving at their stranded friend. Connie stood up—a rolled stripy petal held secure on his back—and aimed to jump through the gap created for him. He landed with a light bounce on the soft, cream leather seat.

"Thank you so much! I had no idea how to wriggle out of there! Can you believe these roses don't have thorns?" Connie told them and they all looked at the flowers. "They did cleverly hide a very pretty string of sparkly stones at the bottom though."

"Oh, that's probably why it was closed up," Loch told Anglo, who nodded agreeingly.

A soft knock on the wind-shield made them look up. It was Rusty, with Lillian and Tuff on her back, pointing towards the palace, where the lady reappeared. The chauffeur shooed at the robin and awaited his passenger with his hand on the door handle.

The Chauns hurried down to the bottom of the door and when it was swung open they leapt onto the step below, only just making it without being squashed by the lady's shoes. Before the engine was started they were safely away from the car on Rusty's back, who kindly flew them to the closest open window to their bunk.

They found the others under their usual cabinet, where they were sat forming a rectangle, passing the peppercorn randomly between each other in silence. The Duo eventually lost their cheer and began sulking about Yeo not letting them go; and Yeo was about to start blaming himself too, with so much time having passed and no sign of their friends. There was still no sign of Ninian, but they were used to only seeing him occasionally.

"Chin up, we are back!" smiled Connie at them before

they could see him.

Elma jumped up and gave Lillian a big hug and the Duo's hard feelings toward Yeo lifted too. Yeo then quickly decided that this must mean he can be the boss again.

"Who wants to play?" he asked picking up the peppercorn.

"Look, Hammy, that's the thing Ninian left here yesterday!" said Hetty. "The one I told you about!"

"So it was Ninian!" Yeo exclaimed and looked at Elma. "I told you I found it!" Elma responded with a tired smile, worrying all day was strangely just as exhausting as the quest that the others undertook.

"Well, there's always tomorrow," said Yeo as he limped towards their secret storage to put the ball away. They took a deep breath and made their way back up to the bunk. Tuff carried Yeo and he was so tired by the end that he snubbed climbing up the lamp too and just collapsed onto the frame.

Connie picked a new yellow petal on the way back to the bunk from one of the bouquets and Lillian shared her reward with Elma; the sweet smelling petal was cosy and warm.

Later, as the exhausted Chauns slept on their bunk,

the relieved employees rushed by and talked about the strange, but lucky way the earring was found.

And if you wonder how that earring
fell but ended up disappearing,

From dusty grounds to leafy skies,
ask what ways lead to such highs?

Was it a bird? It could have been,
finding delight in the golden sheen.

No, that's not likely, and too bold,
as birds don't have a taste for gold.

Was it a squirrel? It must've been
taken while stuck to something green.

Still not convinced? I'm not surprised,
earrings aren't easily disguised.

But no, this is no phoney tale,
It was caught on a squirrel's tail.

Tagged along up in the trees too,
and it fell out there without a clue.

Perhaps none of this would matter
But if it did then all the better.

The Spell

"Hang on," I said. "Wait a moment!
How come with all that movement,
No one ever sees you by chance,
With a well–timed lucky glance?"

"That's easy. I'll tell you how,
If you stared at someone now,
They'd look your way, there is no doubt,
The opposite, for us, works out.

But to no one you must tell,
That looks and glances we repel.
This spell only works if we,
Keep up a constant guard, you see.

When you caught me half off-guard,
My protection was briefly scarred.
A great chance to see me you had,
Only because I was so very sad."

Although now it turned out fine,
I warned him he should hide next time.
In danger I'd hate him to be,
Not everyone is friendly like me.

"Friendly or not, it must be sad,
To be so big is surely bad!
Twelve of us can all be merry
From just one luscious blueberry!

But you'd need mountains of it,
A lot more effort, you must admit!
With your mouth so much wider,
You can't avoid the pesky seeds either!"

It's true, I guess I'd like it all right,
If berries were more than one bite.
Though here I reminded him that,
Fewer things can crush me flat.

He smiled and said it was a tie,
As trees and bushes we passed by,
He cleared his throat and began,
A tale of something lost again.

Spotted

The problem with cleaning days was the early start. Connie had to be woken up, and as it would have been too beastly to assign this task to one particular individual, they did it all together every week. First, they surrounded him forming an open circle, then the Duo poked him. It never woke Connie but it was a fun starting point.

Lillian followed by rubbing his right cheek and Elma joined her rubbing the other side. Connie grunted and pulled his blanket over his head, exposing his feet, which Anglo—being the tallest present—grabbed at once.

Tickling the thick soles of Chaun feet was useless so he hoisted them up in the air, turning Connie upside down. The petal blanket fell on the frame silently and Connie wriggled around with angry sounds before cracking his eyes slightly open.

"Now?" asked Hammy but Tuff shook his head. "Give him a little more time."

"Wake up Connie, it's cleaning day!" Hetty shouted in vain.

"Cleaning days should die!" moaned Connie and

tried to reach his blanket. Tuff grabbed his wrists and swung him side to side with Anglo whilst he carried on with his complaints.

"Cleaning days should perish in perilous perils!" Connie screamed as Tuff looked at Hammy and Hetty. "Try now."

"Hoover!" the pair yelled at Connie's face and, with that, Connie suddenly looked very alert.

"Hoover!" he repeated and he was lowered to the frame from which he jumped up as if it were on fire. He was well and truly awake as he cried, "Run! Run!"

They had to, indeed, for the staff were not far from coming in with the dust-whiskers to dust the frames and other decorative elements above the floor. They chose another cabinet to hide underneath on cleaning days, the closest one on the left side, as the right one— although equally close—doubled up as a secret door.

When the dust removal was all over, and in the short amount of time before hoovering started, they rushed back up to the bunk, far away from their greatest enemy —the dust eaters.

When the room calmed down and people left to take their well deserved breaks, the little Chauns could finally go have some fun. And today something exciting caught Connie's attention.

"I can feel a good breeze coming from the Music Room! If they left a window open accidentally then I think it might just give us the best slide ever designed!"

The Chauns' faces lit up.

"Keep calm," said Yeo. "This needs further thinking!"

"Only because it wasn't your idea," Tuff said. "You have no chance to stop us!"

"Yeah, let's go! I want to try it!" cried Lillian.

"Me too! Quick, whilst we can!" added Elma.

"Bring your blankets for safe landing!" Tuff reminded them.

"No," said Hammy. "I'm not sure I want to try."

"Too scared?" Anglo said, poking fun at him.

"Don't mind him," said Tuff. "Come, we need someone to look out and warn us if ginormees come our way."

Hammy nodded and when they all landed on the floor, he began to head towards the gallery.

"Wait, Hammy," Tuff said. "We need two lookouts. You go cover the Blue Drawing Room whilst Anglo will have the gallery."

"Why me?" Anglo asked, seriously offended.

"Because I heard your voice most recently," Tuff said

curtly. "Random pick."

"Yeah, right," Anglo puffed as he headed towards the long corridor running along the rooms in parallel.

The others made their way towards the Music Room. When they entered it they saw that the bottom half of one window had been left gaping, and between the bordering heavier, red draperies pulled to each side, a light and white curtain drawn across was happily dancing to the tunes of the wind.

"Look, they have the rugs down today for our perfect landing too!" Connie yelled and he was the first to reach the top of the red curtain, but the others weren't far behind, so they all lined up on the curtain rod.

From here, Connie took a sudden jump and down he slid the bouncy slide before eventually being thrust by a sudden gust of wind. He opened his petal and glided through the air with loud shouts of "yippee" and "woo-hoo". Without doubt he was having a tremendous amount of fun so the others didn't hesitate to follow him one by one.

By the time it was Lillian's turn Connie was already up on the rod again, waiting to begin the second round, before Tuff, the last one in the queue had even had his first. The others were still on the parquet floor. Lillian—

fidgeting nervously—seemed to have seconds thoughts, so Connie impatiently told her to hurry up or move. But Lillian did finally jump and she was about to begin to have fun when the echo of fast and sturdy steps suddenly filled the room. Connie looked at the doors in shock, but the plump lady entering was walking so briskly that by the time Lillian was halfway down she was already stepping in front of the curtain. It would have been fine had she not stopped to look at the window as she opened her purse. And just as she did that, Lillian landed in the mouth of the plump lady's bag, which swallowed her at once.

She was soon locked into the darkness with a click when the lady diverted her attention to a member of uniformed staff entering the room.

"I was about to call someone. I could feel the breeze from afar. Do find out who left the window open as it shouldn't be," she said. "I'm in a hurry."

"Yes madam," the man said and made his way to the window to close it as the lady turned around to carry on with her business.

When the window was closed and no one was in the room, silence spread faster than the fresh air did before being cut off. Tuff looked at Connie, Connie looked at the rug. The rug that was empty, the rug Lillian was supposed to land on.

Elma and the others, who scuttled to safety at the skirting, turned to the door. Hammy was standing there, behind the door frame, peeking in with a solemn face.

"It wasn't me!" Anglo cried as he reached the room running.

"Hammy, why didn't you say someone was coming?" Elma yelled at him.

"I…" he began but he struggled with finishing his sentence.

"What is it?" Connie bellowed.

"I was distracted," Hammy muttered. "I'm sorry".

"Distracted?" Connie didn't lower his voice. "With what? Is foraging really more important to you than our safety?"

Hammy shot his eyes down and was too upset to say anything.

"Calm down, it's all going to be fine. She will be brought back soon, I'm sure," Tuff said in a hurried attempt to calm Connie.

But Connie was furious. He slid down on the curtain with incredible friction. Tuff followed him climbing.

"I'm going to find out when," he said curtly, his

palms burning.

"How?" asked Loch and Elma at the same time.

"I'm going to the kitchen," he said with a serious face. "She may have come from there."

"Not the kitchen! There are lots of people there!" whispered Elma.

"I'll come with you!" said Tuff, catching up with Connie now.

"No, you keep the group together and safe," Connie said before he ran off. He knew the kitchen was a dangerous call and a rather far destination, but he had no better idea than to ask the dweller whom he had fleetingly seen there before, during a short adventure to the kitchen. If his guess was correct, then this creature would very much still be there and would no doubt know a few things about the palace employees.

"Poor Lillian!" cried Elma. "It must be awfully dark in there! I do hope she won't be crushed by something heavy."

This thought made the Chauns extremely worried and they didn't know what to do. Soon footsteps could be heard approaching and although no one entered the room, they drew back to under their favourite cabinet until Connie's return. No one noticed that Hammy was not there with them.

Hammy was in the next room, looking for a crying little voice that had distracted him earlier. Now Lillian might be crying as well and he wanted to make sure to at least help this desperate voice. He was just heading towards the fireplace earlier, too, when he noticed the lady passing through the room. He started running back desperately but even a sudden shriek would have been too late to warn them.

This time he reached the fireplace without anyone entering, but he could no longer hear the cry. He was waiting quietly, even held his breath for a while, and maybe such silence helped him pick up on a soft sob, and another one. It was coming from inside the fireplace, of that he was certain. He climbed in to investigate. A tiny little ladybird was hiding there, visibly distressed.

"Are you all right?" asked Hammy. The ladybird jerked at his sudden approach and drew away from him.

"Who are you?" she asked.

"I'm Hammy," the little Chaun said. "I live here and I heard you cry earlier."

"I'm sorry," said the ladybird. "I probably shouldn't be here."

"You are right, you must come out of the fireplace,

it's a very dangerous place to be."

"If you show me an exit I will be able to fly away," the ladybird said.

"I don't think you should leave whilst you are so upset. Perhaps you would like a drink instead?"

"Am I not a bother?" the ladybird asked with a spark of surprise in her voice.

"Of course not! I have friends who live here too, I'm sure they will cheer you up!" Hammy said, forgetting how upset they were with him. The ladybird looked nervous.

"I'm not sure. I don't belong," she said.

"It'll be fine," Hammy said, a little unsure about what she meant.

"You are my guest for now." He smiled at her kindly, which seemed to help ease her worries a bit and she came forward.

When they reached the Chauns' signature cabinet, the others looked at Hammy with a hostile expression before noticing the ladybird. When he told them how he had found her they became curious and Elma stepped closer to introduce herself.

"Hi! I'm Elma," she said and turned around to name the others behind her.

"And these are Hetty, Tuff, Yeo, Anglo, Stoop, Stump and Loch."

They all waved at her and she said, "I don't think I have a name but it's nice to meet you all."

Then Anglo asked, "Are you lost?"

"No. I mean, yes. Actually, I'm not lost but rather, something of mine is," she tried to explain.

"Oh! Is it somewhere in the palace?" asked Loch. "Good luck finding it, this place is huge!"

"I wish it were," sighed the ladybird. "It's one of my spots actually." As she turned around, the Chauns saw her shiny red back had two spots on each side.

"There should be one in the middle, too. I must find it so I can properly belong at home, where everyone has five of them, only I don't. So they told me to go and find it. And I have been searching and searching, but it's been so long that now I am not sure if it's lost, or I never had it to begin with."

The Chauns all looked at each other thinking how horrible those other ladybirds sounded, but smiled at their guest kindly.

"Can we get her something to drink perhaps?" Hammy asked breaking the silence.

Tuff nodded and told five of them to bring some water

from a vase.

"Weo, Weo!" jumped the Duo.

"Then I won't," said Yeo. "I need a break from them."

"Nay, nay!" said the Duo, then grabbed Yeo by the elbow and dragged him away with them. Loch and Hammy followed the tail of wails emanating from Yeo. The concerned looking ladybird was told not to mind them and began to chat with Hetty and Elma whilst Loch and Tuff nervously waited for Connie to return.

Connie had reached the distant kitchen safely. It was bustling and full of people and loud noises. It seemed very confined with furnishings occupying most of the middle in comparison to the long and spacious corridors and rooms elsewhere and, although the grey surfaces gave a cold feel at first impression, the hot steam and lovely smells of cooking filled the room with warmth.

Connie kept very close to the bottom of the cabinets to avoid the cluster of busy feet as he headed towards a little built-in cove with an arched opening at the furthest side of the kitchen. The cove accommodated a very basic but wide and sturdy metal shelving unit.

When he reached it safely, he looked around until he found a skinny spider right behind one of the bars of the shelving unit, peeking out at the energetic kitchen staff.

Someone with short grey hair under his hat was giving lots of instructions at the moment.

"Hello there!" Connie called for his attention. The spider eyed him cautiously.

"What does a leprechaun want from me?" he asked curtly.

"Wow, you are good, knowing about us!" said Connie, genuinely impressed.

"You must be a friend of that other little one with weird ears that often comes to the kitchen at night," the spider said.

"You must mean Ninian," Connie replied. "Yes, we are both Chauns."

"And your business is?" the spider reminded Connie.

"I need to know who was sent out on an errand this morning and when she will be back."

"Why should I know?" the spider replied and turned his head away.

"Oh, come on! We all know why spiders lurk around windows...You are bored and nosy! And the nosiest ones even come inside for full-time surveillance! Like you!"

"I'm not nosy!" the spider growled at Connie. "I'm cultivated. Now off you go," the spider said and shooed him away silently with one of it's legs.

"So you don't know?" asked Connie and looked at him squint-eyed.

"Of course I know. I know everything that goes on around here, but I'm obliged not to tell you. Royals live here. Things must be kept a secret you know," the spider said smugly. But Connie only cared about Lillian at the moment.

"I bet there's one thing you don't know and I could tell you . . . " Connie said with a coy face. "I could tell you what heinous creature tampers with your web when you withdraw."

Connie turned away to face the kitchen staff. "But I guess you will never find out."

"Wait!" said the spider. "Indeed, I don't know what happens when I am not looking, which is a bother. But how would *you* know?"

"Our Ninian is quite cultivated too."

The spider could not have known that Ninian never said anything, but still waited a moment before giving in, stifling a sigh. "They sent a top member of staff out to the Ritz to fetch some saffron. This isn't a usual outing, but it happens every now and then. She must be back before the preparation of lunch finishes, which could be any minute now."

"Thank you! I'm so happy to hear she'll be back soon. The creature that destroys your web is a ginormee," Connie said, pointing at the busy kitchen staff. "They do it in turns."

The spider straight away sent an evil glare towards the staff trying to locate the culprit fitting the description, when realisation struck him.

"You sneak! How is this information useful to me at all? It could be any of them!" he yelled at Connie who was walking away with a distant response, "I never said it was. But you wanted to know!"

Connie made his way back towards the kitchen door carefully and soon saw the lady returning. He watched with his heart in his mouth pounding against his head as she opened her purse and took out the pouch she had brought.

She handed it to one of the cooks as she said, "You are lucky, this was the last one they had."

"We were a bit worried, these are hard to get hold of, very precious indeed," the man with the grey hair said. "They may just keep one reserved for the Palace. They are nice like that at the Ritz."

Connie heard them talk some more but he paid no

attention because he was looking at the purse that was now closed again. There was no sign of Lillian climbing out of it so he was eyeing the plump lady now from head to toe. She might be in a pocket, or on her scarf he thought. But minutes passed and still nothing.

He spoke Lillian's name softly, but there came no response either. So he was sure that Lillian could not be with her at this time and raced back to the White Drawing Room to see if she had landed sooner.

He mounted the staircases fervently, it took so awfully long to climb up the steps one by one compared to jumping down, that it was no surprise they avoided them in general—Ninian had to be crazy to do this with his pocket full at times.

When he reached their usual cabinet the first thing he saw was a ladybird having sips of water from a neatly folded petal cup. She had finished telling stories about her travel and was listening keenly to all the details of Chaun life in the palace. But there was no sign of Lillian.

"Isn't she back yet?" Connie blurted in a rush. "I just saw the lady return to the kitchen!"

"No, nothing yet," said Tuff and his eyes widened. "What could this mean?"

Connie wasn't sure but he didn't have a good feeling

about it. The other Chauns started to look anxious too, so the ladybird asked what was wrong. Elma told her about their morning and Lillian being lost. Then she let out a sudden and short cry.

"Connie! She cannot possibly be still in the purse, right?" she asked with a face that looked like a ghost had tampered with.

"No! Absolutely not!" Connie said and even stamped his feet.

"But what is there for us to do to know for sure?" asked Loch quietly.

"You will all stay here and worry your wits out. I, however, refuse to just sit still. I heard where the lady has been and I am going to go and see if Lillian is there."

"Don't be ridiculous, Connie! Leave the palace grounds?" snapped Yeo.

"Are you insane? You don't even know which way to go!" Tuff said, alarmed at Connie's suggestion.

"I probably do," said the ladybird. They all looked at her. "If you really know where she's been."

"The spider and the maid both said 'the Ritz'! Do you know it?" Connie's eyes were full of hope and anticipation.

"Yes, I know it. It's a hotel on a long street called

Piccadilly. But you couldn't miss it," she said. The Chauns looked at her with admiration and quiet *ohs*. The ladybird felt heartened from the sudden admiration and she carried on in an upbeat tone.

"I have spent so much time browsing London for my lost spot, I learnt all about the maps and the famous places. There are lots of them, they tell you where you are as well as what streets are in walking distance. Of course their 15 minutes is nothing if you fly like I do!"

"Oh, but I don't fly," Connie said and his excitement visibly melted off his face.

"I think I can carry you," said the ladybird. "You don't seem very heavy."

"Really? I'm so glad you are here, even though I am not really sure why or who you might be!" said Connie which made the ladybird flush with happiness. Not that anyone could ever notice.

"We can go whenever. I'll tell you all about it en route," she said.

"Now! Let's go now!" Connie urged. "We just need to find a window that's open."

"Well, out of the 256 windows the palace has, one is bound to be open for sure!" Anglo said jokingly.

"Subtract the upstairs one we never go to," Yeo

corrected him.

"We would if we could fly, which they can, " Loch pointed out.

But they found one not far away and off they flew with the ladybird grabbing Connie by his braces. The others wished them good luck. Connie was light, but the ladybird still needed to rest every now and then, so they had to stop several times.

Connie loved seeing the city from high up and heard all about the lost spot and where the ladybird had come from. He had no problems voicing his opinion.

"They sound utterly and totally unpleasant," he stated with a serious face. "Has it ever occurred to them that they might all have one too many spots? Ask where they stole it from, see how they like that!"

But the ladybird wasn't easy to cheer up so Connie left it at that for now. Fortunately they didn't have to go far, and soon they reached their destination. When they saw the side door being opened for someone, they quickly made their way inside.

Connie wasn't sure what to expect, but this was most certainly nothing like he could have imagined. The place was very big, although a lot smaller than the palace. It felt everlastingly warm and spacious, with numerous mood lights and big chandeliers.

The interior had a dominant white and golden theme that was accented by intense shades of reds in the long corridor. Patterns and decorative details featured on the tall walls and the very many people gave a busy and important feel to the hotel. Some of them were standing at the front desks talking, whilst others were sitting down. Many wore dark uniforms with white stripes, and a few of these rushed by pushing carts of luggages. The ladybird flew to a chandelier in the middle of the corridor and they had a rest there.

"How will we find Lillian? I don't even know where to look," panicked Connie.

"Do you know what she came here for?" asked the ladybird.

"Saffron for the Palace chef I think," said Connie.

"Then we should probably find out if they have a kitchen here as well," said the ladybird and looked around. "I'll fly around and see what is within reach. Wait for me here, will you?"

Connie nodded and the ladybird flew off. Whilst she was away a young lad in uniform appeared, carrying a large white plate mostly covered with a silver dome. He was going to walk under the chandelier and Connie wondered if he should attempt to jump onto his thick and curly dark hair.

It felt like a chance that might not come again, he looked like kitchen staff. Connie looked around anxiously to see if the ladybird was back yet but he didn't see her.

He did see, however, specks of light flicker in a distant corner. For a moment his gaze was captivated by the tiny dots floating around slowly and the passing moments made his heart sink when he realised he had missed more than he could make up for. Indeed, the young lad was long gone but Connie's spirit came back as he spotted the ladybird returning. He wanted to tell her to look at the odd lights but when he looked again they were gone and the corner looked perpetually still. Strange, he thought, but then the ladybird spoke.

"I found the kitchen," she said and grabbed Connie. The kitchen was really close, but it was hidden behind many swing doors. When—with good timing—they finally got through all of them, the ladybird lowered Connie to the centre counter-top.

"Stay on this one whilst I fly around quickly," she said. "You are less noticeable anyway."

This kitchen felt cold with the dominating greys of metallic surfaces, which shone like the morning frost of wintry days. He called Lillian's name—low and careful—hoping she would hear and respond. He walked around, unknowingly towards a hob that had been turned on in advance for heat. A moment later a pan with oil in it was quickly placed on, heating up fast enough for the tossed in fish to splatter hot oil on Connie's shoulder.

"Ouch!" he bellowed, to which the cook jumped back and into another cook, who dropped a plateful of beautifully assembled food, that was ready to be served.

The battered fish sizzled in the pan and that was the only sound following the sharp echo of shattering plate. For a moment everyone silently wondered if there was merit in picking it up, after all it was wasted time, for now they had to create that dish again.

Someone then grabbed a broom with a wide head and pushed it all into a corner to be dealt with later. Work at once resumed as if nothing had happened. Connie watched the events unfold and didn't notice Lillian walking up behind him.

"Connie! What are you doing here?" Lillian asked sounding surprised, but the faint smile on her face revealed that she was glad to see him.

"Lillian!" Connie spun around startled. He was still rubbing his shoulder but the pain soon went away and the hot oil left no permanent damage.

"I've come to find you!" he said. "We were really worried about you!"

"I know! I'm sorry. When I saw light I quickly climbed out to look around. It looked like she was to stay for a few minutes so when I saw some cakes being decorated with walnut pieces, I went to grab one but she suddenly left and so I had no choice but to hide."

"Really, Lillian. Walnuts?" Connie scolded her. "There's plenty at the palace I'm sure!"

"But we never go to the kitchen and I promised some for Rusty!" Lillian argued.

"Forget it," Connie said curtly. "Ask Ninian."

"Connie, please! Look, they are not that far from here! I want to get some for Rusty myself!"

Connie looked at the end of the kitchen counter. The cakes were no longer there but some walnut pieces were left behind on a wooden board. Connie said no again.

"You are so difficult!" Lillian scoffed.

"I'm not the one who wants walnuts instead of going back!" Connie retorted.

"I want to go back *with* walnuts!" cried Lillian.

"And you call me difficult?" asked Connie.

"Yes! You are fine chasing imaginary cherries on tall winter trees, but you wouldn't go for walnuts we are this close to?"—Lillian extended her right arm towards the board to indicate proximity—"Why?"

Connie didn't reply; arguing was pointless it seemed. "Fine then. Let's try."

They ran to the walnuts, carefully avoiding the hob. Lillian chose a small piece she could tie up on her head with her locks. They both jumped when a ginormee's hand slapped on the surface not far from them.

"Get that bug out of my kitchen!" screamed the head chef. "Now! Before it squirts something on one of my plates!"

Assistants grabbed cutlery and bowls to get rid of the ladybird flying around. The ladybird quickly grabbed Connie and flew him to the shoulder of a very still man, wisely ignoring the bug hunt and drawing delicate lines slowly on a plate with golden caramel sauce. Then she went back for Lillian.

"You must be Lillian," she said. "Sorry, but we need to leave at once."

But Lillian and the walnut were too much for the ladybird.

"I can make it to that plate," said Lillian. "You should go and hide under his collar or something!"

The ladybird nodded and flew back to where she left Connie. The number of staff looking for her quickly reduced to one, a lady who was eyeing the air without blinking, slowly turning clockwise. But she missed the final flight of the ladybird, who was now safely still under a collar with Connie.

After a good run Lillian also managed to jump onto the uniform and when the plate was ready, it was taken out, just not by the man decorating it.

"What do we do now?" asked Lillian. "We are still in here!"

"Discuss why they don't have any windows in this kitchen!" growled the ladybird.

"The ones that come and go stay for too short of a time for all of us to make it," observed Connie. "You should fly onto one of them and Lillian and I can make it through the doors when they are opened."

Lillian agreed and began climbing down on the clothes. Connie followed, telling the ladybird to meet at the long corridor just outside the kitchen. The ladybird waited for the door to open and moved fast when someone entered.

"There it is!" screamed the woman hunting for it. "It's gone, it's gone!" she cheered happily as the spotted beetle disappeared in the doorway. Once out in the long corridor, the ladybird hid on a bouquet of flowers to wait for Connie and Lillian, who were slowed down by the walnut on top of Lillian's head.

"I told you 'no'!" said Connie. "I bet you wish you'd left it!"

"If I did, I would have left it. I could leave it anywhere!" replied Lillian gruffly.

"That's a good idea, leave it right here then," answered Connie.

"No," Lillian said curtly. "Are you finally going to tell me what's your problem?"

"I hate walnuts!" blurted Connie and gave Lillian a cold, hard look.

"Why?"

"You should know they make me *brupple* weird!"

"But it's not for you to eat!" Lillian said in confusion.

"I don't care. I hate them," Connie insisted.

"What's a 'brupple'?" The ladybird asked when she joined them after seeing that they reached the corridor.

"It's what happens after we eat something. We exhale it as vapour with a short squeak. But for Connie, it doesn't go away for a while after eating walnuts and he just carries on squeaking for hours. It's funny really, just not for him."

As Lillian explained, Connie gave her a glare which called for further quarrel. Soon the ladybird was fed up with it and told them, "If you carry on I'll leave you two here and tell the others you have moved. There are plenty of picture frames here for you to sleep on."

The pair walked in silence following that. After hitch-hiking through the revolving main doors they were out in the open air.

"And? What now?" asked Lillian. "How are we to go back all together?"

"We'll carry on walking!" said Connie proudly and they all began moving forward slowly.

"We aren't far but it will be a lot longer on foot," warned the ladybird. The smaller the feet one has to walk on the longer and bigger streets and parks become, which Lillian quickly took notice of.

"It'll take ages! I can't run here, there are feet to break our speed everywhere!"—Her face looked elongated as she looked around in disbelief—"And what if we are too late to make it inside?"

"Then we'll sleep outside," Connie said casually. Lillian sped her steps up.

"Let's craft a song to pass time!" Connie added.

"Please don't tell me that we'll walk and sing about walking!" pleaded Lillian.

"No, that would be boring. We'll sing about..." Connie began and paused for a moment as he looked ahead of him. "This street!"

"This street?" asked Lillian unimpressed.

"Yes. What was it called again?" asked Connie from the ladybird.

"Piccadilly," came the answer.

Connie thought for a little and then some more, murmuring lots and lots to himself before finally speaking out loudly,

"On this street called Piccadilly,
I cannot help but seem silly,
Asking what's a Piccadilly?

Is it tiny? Is it big?
Is it something you can pick?
If you touch it does it prick?

Is it common? Is it rare?
Is it something you can share?
A dilly-dimply kind of pear?

A dilly pear cannot be green,
It's spiky with no waxy sheen,
unsuitable for all cuisine.

A dilly pear cannot be yellow,
with no flesh it's plain and hollow,
Sweet dreams it may even harrow.

A pear so freaky is no pear,
A new title it must bear,
I think I had a word to spare,

Oh yes, I know! Piccadilly,
And although it sounds silly,
There *is* a street called Piccadilly!

And

On this street called Piccadilly… "

"We are not on the street any more!" Lillian interrupted. "You took too long!"

Connie looked around. "Oh, really? And what's the name of this park?" he tried to ask but the others didn't wait around to answer that question, and by the time he uttered the last syllable Lillian and the ladybird were way ahead of him.

"Never mind then," he said casually and ran after them enjoying the open space leading them to the tall garden walls of the palace.

"Hopefully we can drop off the walnut in the garden," suggested Lillian as she climbed slowly with the additional weight. The ladybird helped them each in turn on the way down from the wall—although with Lillian it was more of an easing the fall kind of help—and when they landed they felt relieved and finally free of worries. As they ran ahead they did find Rusty hopping around happily on the sunlit grass. She looked up when she heard Lillian shouting "Rusty! I've got your walnut!"

Lillian released the piece of nut and put it on the soil. The robin picked it up happily.

"It's roasted! Delicious, thank you," she said. Lillian was very happy and started jumping and cheering, "It's so good to be back Rusty! I'm just so relieved! Oh—" she stopped suddenly. "You don't know I was lost for half a day!"

Rusty shook her head and Lillian quickly filled her in. They introduced the ladybird who was very reluctant to come out from among the grass.

"Rusty is fine, she won't try and eat you I promise," Connie reassured her. The robin soon left and as the trio turned around to head to the palace Elma jumped on Lillian, laughing.

"You are safe!" Elma cried. "Oh, we were so worried about you!"

"I told you I heard her voice!" Hetty said proudly.

"What are you guys doing out here?" asked Connie in awe.

"We couldn't just sit about, it was driving us mad!" said Tuff. "So we went to find some ladybirds to see how many spots they had. We left Yeo and Anglo behind though. We met a few and most of them had just two but another had seven—"

"Seven!" exclaimed the ladybird.

"Yeah, so you shouldn't worry about it, but if you do we think we might have found something—" Elma was about to say but Stoop and Stump cut her off.

"No! This is not how you are meant to break good news. Surprise needs to be served better. Watch how it's done!" said Stoop proudly and clapped fast with his fingers as Stump stepped forward.

"Ahem," he cleared his throat and straightened up, raising his chin. "Ready?"

"You wouldn't believe, no you wouldn't," and he paused for impact with a triumphant smile but before his mouth opened to form the sound "*th-*" the ladybird spoke, interrupting the speech.

"Bravo! You can speak normally!" she cheered.

The Duo froze with a chilling glare. They were not done with their recital yet. Stump attempted to carry on once more but this time Tuff was faster.

"They can, but they don't when Yeo is about," he explained. "So most of the time they choose not to."

"Why?" asked the ladybird bemused.

"It winds him up," Connie said with a chuckle. "He doesn't know they are doing it on purpose."

"Why doesn't someone tell him?" the ladybird asked warily. Connie drew closer to the ladybird and whispered in her ear. "We tried, but Yeo thought we were the ones teasing him. I guess he will have to learn to ignore it when he wants to."

"Hello?" the Duo said gruffly. "Can we finish now please?"

"It would be much better if she could see the spot at the same time," suggested Hammy, causing the Duo's patience to crack almost audibly.

"Thanks," they snorted. "For ruining the surprise!" they shouted back as they marched off sulking.

"You found my spot?" asked the ladybird and her wings fluttered momentarily with joy. "Where?"

"Um," began Tuff, "It's a possibility. Come with us."

They took eager steps towards the trees. The Duo stayed behind to sulk but it was no fun without the audience, so they followed the others with some delay.

When the group reached the trees they looked for a specific one that had lots of small holes on it.

"Look, up there!" said Hetty pointing up high at its trunk. "We climbed up to check it from close but you'll have a better view flying."

"But those are holes carved by the great woodpecker!" said Lillian doubtfully.

"All of them? Are you sure? Like *century-certain?*" Loch asked with a serious face.

"Nah, I guess not that much," Lillian replied tamely.

"One in the middle is such a perfect circle and perhaps not deep enough!" said Elma. "Go on, have a look!"

The ladybird flew up to inspect it closely.

"That's a bit of an odd one among them, indeed," she said when she came back. "But I can't put it on my back."

"Maybe it wants you to stay here," Hammy said happily with a wink. "You could use the big one next to it as a home."

The ladybird smiled. "Perhaps you are right. Perhaps it is time for me to stop looking."

"There is nothing but treasures to find in and near Buckingham Palace!" Connie stated proudly.

"Though I really enjoyed my journey," the ladybird

began whilst gazing up at the holes on the tree. "Wait...
I *really* enjoyed my journey! Forget the spot, I'm glad I
don't have one and began to travel!"

"There you go," said Lillian. "You are the one better
off!"

"I am!" danced the ladybird. "I'm off to see more!
Thanks for everything but I really feel like I must go at
once!"

The Chauns waved after her as her tough, armoured
body flew away weightlessly for further adventures.

"No!" the Duo cried, just catching up now. "You can't
ruin the ending! You were meant to stay and listen to
our perfect finale of the day!"

"I guess we'll have to do," Lillian told them with a
kind smile. "Say it to your hearts' content."

And the Duo did, so much so that they wouldn't stop
repeating themselves until they all had reached their
bunk to rest, going:

"You wouldn't believe, no you wouldn't,
That we found the thing you couldn't.

A spot of yours, that ran off one day,
Causing you great dismay.

Your search was frantic, days went past
But your trip ends here at last!

Come, be glad you didn't quit,
As it made you strong and fit.

Though this spot is here to remain,
It comes with a new home to reign.

Like it or not, sorry to say,
"No change or returns, nay nay!"

The Dark Float

"Pause," I said, "it makes no sense,
That the Duo can make Yeo so tense,
He has to know there was a time,
before this started, when they spoke fine.
He must've heard them, there had to be
something to start this tendency!"

"Yes, there was a reason to sulk,
which I think was Yeo's sleep-talk.

Back in the vase during the Dark Float,
He kept repeating the very same note.
When they fell asleep, in their dream,
They were haunted by one repeating scream.

The nightmare note I'll now quote,
Is one that Yeo unknowingly wrote:
'There is a place for "a" in neatly,
But there is none in definitely.
Learn the word preposterous,
It isn't at all monstrous,
And spell well indefinitely.'

This fancy ear-worm straight from hell,
Made them not want to spell well.
But Yeo didn't seem to recall,
The note that nearly caused a brawl.
So they taught him some new words,
Tailored to upset wordy nerds.

The first was "*postros*" uttered with ease,
But Yeo screamed and stuffed his ears.
Then Ninian tried to say something,
But no sound his mouth could bring.

So Yeo assumed that the identical two
Had both lost some verbal skills too.

Our early days are still a haze,
I can only call it a foggy phase,
So I don't have stories from there.
Like not remembering a nightmare,
You want to but just can't recall,
The details of what did befall."

I had something to tell him as well
About this item a man used to sell,
In his home called Pikaddilly Hall,
Where piccadills were sought by all.
A broad, lacy collar for clothes,
Brought the name by which the street goes.

He didn't like it not one bit
asked if I had lost my wit.
A shop described as pikaddilly?
Not unless windows are silly!
I tried to argue, he shook his head,
and told another story instead!

Trial

"This is the best game you've introduced so far Yeo," said Loch with a delighted face and Anglo hummed in agreement as he lifted his club up in the air with an elegant curve, eyeing the semi-transparent little rock before him.

But Yeo wasn't happy about it. He shot an angry look at them.

"I never taught you to catapult salt into people's teas!" he said looking up at Anglo, who was standing higher on the top of a protruding swirl element of the embellished frame.

"Nice shot, Anglo!" clapped Loch when the little rock went flying towards the guests. "Top score for the small milk jugs!"

Anglo and Loch laughed hard.

"Really, that is just so rude!" Elma scolded them. "You simply shouldn't!"

But the guests in the White Drawing Room didn't realise the offence committed against their English teas and all evidence vanished quickly in the warm liquid.

Anglo and Loch were not the only ones having the time of their life, the Duo already had gone through

their salt ammo and were now thinking of other things they could hit with their clubs. Yeo turned his back at them and walked to the other side of the frame, where Connie and Lillian were passing the rock between them, aiming for it to slide through a tight little gap made between two rolled petals laid in a straight line.

"Now *that* is how it ought to be done," said Yeo pointing at them. "Or like that!" He added, pointing at Hammy and Hetty who were just playing catch-ball with it, for there were only eight splints of wood greeting them this morning.

"How many times do you think Ninian had to return to bring all these up here?" asked Hammy.

"I don't know, his pocket is huge!" Hetty, who sewed it, said with a proud smile.

"He must be the fittest of us," said Elma.

"After Tuff, of course," Lillian added, glancing at him with a smirk but Tuff didn't seem to mind.

"He is mad," Anglo said. "To do this for nothing."

"Or just nice," Yeo said who was always very happy with Ninian's little gifts. "Nice, unlike you four, who don't play nicely."

The Duo rolled their eyes.

"Stop doing that with your eyes or you'll stretch them

to the point they fall out!" Yeo yelled at them. "And no 'no ways'!" he added.

"Do we know how long they are staying?" asked Connie, trying to smooth Yeo's angry face and gently knocked the salt at his feet three times before sending it towards the narrow and small gate. His face morphed slightly into a discontented ruffle as he watched the sliding rock miss the target. He walked up to the rock at halt to retrieve it.

"No, we don't. It's not only tea though, it's tea and biscuits. Biscuits!" said Yeo and then frowned anyway.

"Biscuits! Yum!" said Hetty as she looked at the tray but Tuff, who was sitting at the edge of the frame looking for a chance for them to go out, warned her.

"No chance, there are dogs in the next room and the doors are open."

"Shame," said Hammy with a disappointed face. "I bet they will clear up any crumbs, too."

"Good!" said Yeo. "I don't want those cursed things near me."

"Remind me what his problem is with biscuits again?" asked Lillian.

"They are not cakes," replied Connie.

"That's all?"

"No, that's not it," interrupted Yeo, rolling his eyes. "Biscuits are lifeless cakes. They are flat, dried out, dead cakes."

The Duo said something long and undecipherable but Yeo knew perfectly well what they meant.

"They won't fall out, all right? I know that's not how it works," he said and crossed his arms.

"Look! She's dipping it in her tea!" cried Anglo. "Resurrection of the dead cake!"

The Duo cracked up and Yeo covered his face with his palms in horror, muttering something like 'dear me, soggy dead cake' so he couldn't see that no one in fact was dunking their biscuits in tea at Buckingham Palace—an act that had the glorious status of 'never done if never witnessed' there.

"Guys! They are closing the doors! Get ready to head down!" Tuff suddenly called out.

"Finally!" cried the group and abandoned all equipment to line up at the edge.

"Now!" said Tuff. "Everyone, climb fast!"

They never parachuted in people's presence. But so long as the dogs were not around to sniff them out they sneaked around groups easily, especially when their dangerous feet were constrained in the vicinity of their resting hips and ongoing chatter.

"Maybe we can play that egg hunt Yeo said about the other day," suggested Hetty.

"Like when they hid those tiny shiny eggs all over the palace?" asked Hammy.

"Yes, and some very pretty ones too," Hetty replied.

"But we don't have any of those eggs," Loch pointed out.

"Anything will do, it's the kind of hide-and-seek where you don't try and find someone but something of that person's," Yeo explained.

"Are you sure they are not completely different games?" asked Tuff.

"Yes. Everyone has a target object to find and if they find the wrong object—or the wrong egg if it's an egg—then they have to leave it and carry on searching," Yeo explained further.

"What if they take it to collect as many as possible instead?" asked Anglo with a semi-suppressed smirk.

"They'll get biscuits!" Connie said and the group laughed. Yeo sighed and ignored them by thinking of items suitable for today's game. When they reached the floor they were startled to hear the doors being opened again and the dogs' collars chime as they approached.

The Chauns quickly raced for an open window, and went outside as the dogs followed sniffing, stopping confused near the curtains, before heading to the trolleys with treats.

The Chauns didn't go far outside, for despite the sun's presence, dark clouds seemed to be drawing near. They stopped at the bottom of some bushes nearby.

"Now, everyone should go and find something that will be their item, and bring it back here so that we can begin the game. Be back by noon or we will start without you!"

"No biscuits for them," said Anglo and quickly ran off without waiting for Yeo's response.

"Anyone saying biscuit is disqualified from now on!" said Yeo.

"Sounds tempting," Loch muttered and followed Anglo.

"Go, and come back straight away if it starts raining!" Yeo said loudly and walked off alone. Tuff left with Hetty and Hammy, the Duo followed Anglo and Loch, and Elma joined Lillian and Connie for the hunt.

Lillian and Elma walked ahead of Connie, who was deep in thought searching for items that are both unique and easy to notice during a search. Most things he thought of, however, like small rocks and splints of wood, had plenty of them lying around so this was a hard nut to crack. He wondered what the others would come up with and wanting to exceed them made thinking a little more exciting.

After they had crossed the hedge they decided to head left instead of the usual right. They wouldn't go so far as the lake, but maybe this way they would find some new, interesting items that could help them with the game.

The lawn stretched further this side without paths or trees breaking its monotony. Not that they had the sight of the endless vastness, for them the imbalanced soil terrain nourishing the lawn was a world of adventure of its own. But they hadn't made it far when Connie looked to the side and saw the golden flecks floating nearby among the grass, almost staring at him. He stopped, but they disappeared as if the depth of the grass-jungle sucked them in with a quick, gluttonous breath.

"Did you guys see that?" he asked but Lillian and Elma were both so immersed in advancing that they failed to notice Connie stopping. He yelled after them, staring at the spot where the flecks vanished, but couldn't wait patiently so he charged ahead and into the depth, attempting to tail the golden mystery.

Lillian and Elma just about caught a glimpse of the direction in which he headed when they turned back to answer his call, and ran after him at once.

"What is it Connie? Why did you change direction?" asked Lillian as they caught up with him.

"I saw something strange," Connie replied, rooted to the spot and looking around keenly. "It could still be around."

"What is it we are looking for?" asked Elma.

"Little golden lights hovering," Connie explained. Lillian and Elma looked at him with barefaced doubt.

"I know, they are gone," Connie said, looking vexed. "Let's just carry on anyway."

As they walked on, the thin and soft stalks of the grass thickened up so they changed direction again, heading towards a broad and open space, where a honey bee was hopping fast on elastic legs, punching the air vehemently with strong and fast blows.

"Whoa," said Lillian. "I didn't know bees do that!"

"We don't unless the circumstances call for practice," said the bee but didn't turn around, just kept his left arm punching forward straight a few times, then suddenly a right hook was inserted. Connie thought the bee meant business and he was glad to be standing behind him.

"You seem good already," he said.

"Not compared to that annoying wasp. Need to win the duel," he said and glanced at them for a brief moment then carried on facing away again. "He offended our Queen. He said us bees were fake wasps that turned out wrong hence we are hairy."

"How dare he!" exclaimed Elma. "Bees are honey-bosses no one should mess with!" The golden greatness was a favourite treat of hers, as it was for most Chauns.

"He is quite big and intimidating," said the bee.

"Just ignore him, he is clearly wrong," said Connie, but the bee didn't welcome the idea. He stopped to face Connie; his front right leg curled up into a fist with such force Connie could almost see smoke emerge from it. He wished he hadn't spoken.

"Put up with it forever, you mean? No thanks, how would you feel if you were mocked by a fairy for being a weird elf?"

"We're leprechauns, actually," Connie said with the strange combination of a hurtful squint and a friendly smile.

"Well, you corrected me because it does matter. Thanks for proving my point, now go away and leave me be."

Connie stayed silent and Lillian gently tried pulling him away from the bee, whilst mumbling apologies.

"When is the duel?" Connie asked quickly before going.

"A bit later," the bee said, and took a quick look at the sky. "I actually don't have much time left if you don't mind. "

"And where—" Connie began, but Lillian grabbed him this time with a strong pull.

"Come on, Connie!"

"Good luck and be safe," Connie said but the bee didn't pay attention to them any more as they walked off towards the grass blades to pursue their original aim.

"I don't really want him to fight the wasp," Connie said to Lillian.

"I know, but you can't stop him, you saw how upset he was!" she replied.

"Quite rightly as well, that nasty wasp should take it all back and apologise!" Elma said gruffly.

"But what if the bee tries to sting the wasp?" asked Connie. "Don't they die after that?"

"Do they?" asked Elma alarmed.

"I'm not sure," said Lillian. "I did hear something about it."

"I hope that was just a scary story for Halloween," Elma said with a shudder.

"It's not worth the risk though," Connie said, as he kicked a tiny pebble. It hopped around and disappeared among the sparse grass stalks, before eventually coming to rest with an "*ouch*".

"That wasn't some sort of a bug I just kicked, was it?" Connie asked, concerned.

"I don't think so. But let's go and check!" Lillian said.

They followed the route the pebble took, and as they did they heard more voices—becoming louder and clearer as they unwittingly approached another open space.

"Silence! The audience are to remain silent at all times!" said a deep, authoritative voice.

"Someone threw a stone at me!" cried another voice.

"It wasn't me!" one yelled.

"Me either!" came a response followed by a similar one, "No use looking at me!"

"Quiet! Can we get back to the present matter please?" said the same authoritative voice, making it more of an instruction than a question. The crowd gradually quietened down, and as the Chauns carefully proceeded forward they soon caught a view of the gathering. They hid behind a thick grass stalk at the edge of the lawn bordering a small, bald area of soil, filled with a large group of tiny snails.

Although they were immersed in the events, one of them—presumably the unlucky one who was hit—kept on cautiously glancing towards the grassy area on the side, where the Chauns were standing. There were two of them in the front, facing the crowd—one looked irate and the other upset—and another higher up, clinging to a leaf that lowered him enough to tower above the crowd and address them.

"As we agreed so far, both of them can't possibly own the same home," the snail on the leaf, who had the authoritative voice, said. "But they both claim to have a right to it and right now, they both have traces indicating presence at some point."

"That one's lying!" shouted a snail and pointed at the one on the right.

"No, it's the other one for sure!" cried another.

"Silence! Silence!" the snail in charge raised his voice. "No prejudice! We'll find out the truth soon. Let's begin with the questions!" The snails roared and the little Chauns became increasingly curious.

"Let's sit behind them and watch this!" whispered

Connie.

"But what if they tell us off and send us away?" Elma muttered.

"Well, we will stand up, come back here and watch them all the same," replied Connie, still whispering.

"No, we are staying here, let's not disturb them again," Lillian said quietly as she had her stare fixed on the gathering. Connie and Elma sat down and listened in silence.

"So you say the home is yours," began the snail in charge, looking at the upset one. "How come he knows it so well?" he asked as he orientated his eyes towards the irate snail.

"He forced me out," began the upset one. "One day he knocked on my door and asked what that sign on the outside was about. I told him I had no signs anywhere, but he insisted I should look. So I did and as I went outside he sneaked in and shut me out!"

"I only did that because he was living in my house!" the irate snail said defiantly. "He seemed to have moved in whilst I was away travelling, so I had to lure him out to claim my property back!"

"Quiet!" roared the questioner. "I'll get to you shortly." He turned back to the first snail.

"His description of the place had more details, which would imply a higher level of affection and a greater amount of time spent living there."

"He planned this from the start so I guess he knew you'd ask and I didn't," the upset snail tried to defend himself.

"And can you prove that?"

"No, I can't," replied the snail and he became even more upset. The snail in charge carried on asking questions regarding when the home was set up, and what kind of environment it was made in. He also enquired about whether any guests or friends stayed or visited who could point out the true owner. The answers were the same from both, so the problem was no closer to resolution yet.

"How can they argue about their homes being the same? They each have their own on their back!" Lillian said loudly to Connie, who shrugged.

"Who is there? Show yourself at once!" the snail in charge said and the crowd stared at the grass. Lillian, Connie and Elma slowly and reluctantly emerged from among the grass stalks.

"They threw the rock at me!" yelled a snail in the middle of the crowd. "Enemy!"

"No, I kicked it and it hit you by accident, I'm sorry," Connie said.

"You are lucky it didn't crack my hut or you'd meet my finest slime-ball in return!"

"Your hut? You mean the shell on your back?" asked Lillian. The snail nodded.

"I knew it! Then what home are you arguing about? Don't you each have one on your back?" she asked. The snails looked at her as if her last words were uttered in code.

"That's the stupidest question I have ever been asked," came the answer. The others bounced their flexible eyes in agreement, which made them look like a hostile troop of bouncy balls.

"Do we look like we want to trail along and sleep in mud all the time? Excuse me, but we have standards thank you very much," said the snail in charge and gave Lillian a piercing glare.

"So all of you have an extra home somewhere?" Connie asked bemused. The snails hummed and jiggled their eyes in harmony to concur with the statement.

"And has something like this never happened before?"

Contrary to Connie's expectations, the snails did not

shake their heads. He surmised that it would make their eyes tangle too much, which would be a struggle to undo. Perhaps they learnt it the hard way and, as he imagined it, he pulled silly faces trying to conceal a smile.

"Not that I know of," said the snail in charge. "Hence one of them is a liar and a thief."

"So how about this," Connie began, "since it's not needed all the time there might be other snails who use it too, you just don't know because they leave by the time you come back. In this case, however, they unfortunately met."

"Not possible!" said the snail in charge. "We would see the slime. We would know it's not ours."

"Are you sure?" Lillian asked bravely. "It looks all the same to me." The snails gave her the same uncomfortable stare for the second time.

"I don't like your friend," a snail said looking at Connie. "I bet it was her who kicked the rock really."

The snail on the leaf sighed. "We would know, yes," he said patiently.

"Do you never clean it up?" Lillian said, further braving out the hostility.

She expected another round of bored frowns but the snails broke out in uncontrollable laughter.

"You heard that?" said a snail amidst laughing.

"Yeah, she said clean—" began another but couldn't finish because much like most other snails, laughing so hard made him retract back into his shell, which rocked back and forth with the giggles. Lots of rocking snail shells was a sight that left the three Chauns speechless.

"Of course we don't, then it would look like it's empty and available!" the snail on the leaf said. He was not laughing, he was starting to lose patience with being asked questions instead of asking them, like it had been intended before the Chauns barged in.

"I do," said the upset looking snail.

"Me too," admitted the irate one as well.

"You do what?" asked the snail in charge and turned to them. "Are you dumb?"

The irate looking snail began to look upset hearing that, and the upset looking one became irate instead.

"I don't want to come back to it looking all slimy!" said the now irate one.

"And covered in *trodadoodle*," added the other.

"All right, I think it's obvious now what happened," said the snail on the leaf. "But this makes it impossible to decide which one of you should give it up."

Connie, now zealous with the immense discovery,

was eager for a conclusion.

"They can share!" he said. "Sharing is fun, right?"

Elma and Lillian nodded and they all instinctively began chanting their sharing anthem.

"Sharing is not just good for cheese,
Not just to be nice or to please,
But for super flavour release!

Break and share for a good reason:
It's always the best method to season,
Selfishness is the biggest treason!

The smallest broken piece is the best,
We race for that before the rest,
If we get it we are filled with zest!

When the small ones have all gone,
The last big one we set upon,
To split, so sharing carries on

Because,
Sharing is not just.... "

The snails didn't sing along. They looked at them puzzled and then one of them asked, "What's cheese?"

The Chauns looked at each other, struggling to come up with an adequate description, which the snails would understand.

"Cheese is food you can share!" Elma tried.

"Actually, so are some snails I believe," said Connie in a low voice, but fortunately the snails didn't hear him.

"I don't want to share!" said the irate snail.

"Me either!" added the other one.

"Well, if you don't want to share, then I say the upset one keeps the place," Connie chose randomly.

"I was upset first!" shouted the irate snail and became upset again.

"Prove it, you liar!" barked the upset snail irately.

"As if such things could be proved!" came the defence.

Now both snails looked angry and it was impossible to tell who was the original grump.

"Without proof no damage can be acknowledged," said the snail in charge. "Who complained first about being forced out? The other keeps the place if the claimant has no clear evidence."

"That's not fair either!" Lillian moaned. "Surely there is something better to come up with? That one might be a fraud, we don't know the truth yet!"

"Well, you don't know what you can't know," said the snail on the leaf as he started to crawl down. "It's either this, decided based on evidence, they argue forever or they settle."

"Come on," began Lillian tenderly. "You don't need it at the same time and it's useful that the other looks after the place whilst one is gone, especially if it looks vacant once it's cleaned."

The snails looked at each other and their stiff expressions softened slightly.

"I guess," began one, "I could try to learn to live with it."

"We could try, but no promises!" said the other.

"Case dismissed!" cheered the snail in charge and the crowd burst into hurrays.

Soon they all started to leave and so did Connie, Lillian and Elma. But they still thought about all they had seen and heard instead of Yeo's game.

"I know!" Connie cried suddenly. He looked up at the sky. "We can stop the fight! We must hurry!" And he turned around to race back to where they met the bee.

"Connie! Wait!" shouted Elma and Lillian but the Chaun didn't stop or wait so they ran after him. Connie reached the spot with incredible speed but the bee was no longer hopping around. Luckily he was still there though, halfway sucked into a flower.

"Hello again!" Connie said bravely and the bee climbed out. "Having a spot of lunch?"

"Not just, I love the smell so much, it relaxes me," the bee replied. "I have to leave in a minute and I am rather nervous."

"Take me with you!" Connie said. "I can help you settle this once and for all!"

The bee eyed him with suspicion.

"We want to come too!" Elma said as she arrived with Lillian. "Connie, stop running off alone!"

"I don't think there is much you can do, the wasp would just further mock me for needing company," the bee said.

"Just try it, I promise it will be fine," Connie tried to convince him. "All you need to do is repeat to him what I say on your back when you see him. If we hide on your back he might not even see us!"

"All right then," the bee said softly as he felt secretly happy for the last minute company.

The three of them climbed on the bee's back and found it very cosy with the soft hair covering the insect.

"Just don't pull it too hard," the bee warned them and they were very cautious not to.

It was a long, but amazing ride. The bee was buzzing softly like a tiny and delicate machine, and the fresh wind brushed their skin where it wasn't stroked by the bee's warm and luscious hair.

The wasp was already waiting for the bee at the furthest end of the garden, on top of the walls. It did look big and strong. The bee slowly lowered itself and took a position ready for defence. Elma was starting to freak out but Lillian looked at her and raised her index finger to her mouth so she kept it to herself. Only Connie made a sound as he whispered to the bee's ears.

"W-w-we," stuttered the bee but then gathered some courage when Elma gave him a gentle hug.

"We n-need to talk," he said repeating exactly what Connie whispered behind him.

"Got cold feet, yellow zebra?" sneered the wasp.

"What a fork," said the bee, mishearing Lillian's mutters labelling the wasp a dork. Connie gave her a mild *twinch*, a Chaun warning carried out by forming a tweezer with their fingers to pinch and pull their incredibly tight skin, which effectively zipped her mouth.

"What did you say?" asked the wasp furiously.

"I said don't bark," said the bee repeating what Connie came up with to rectify the situation.

"Oh, you are so cool now telling me what to do!"

"I'm not scared of you. Your words are nothing but brupples! There's no lasting substance to it!" said the bee relaying Connie's words.

"I don't know what a brupple is, but I know you are just a plain wasp wannabe!"

"Prove it!" said the bee.

"Prove what?" asked the wasp.

"Prove that I am a fake wasp!" came the response. The wasp was taken aback. Connie felt ecstatic again. He turned to Lillian and whispered with a wink, "You don't know what you can't know."

"You don't what know," repeated the bee struggling to pick up all of it what Connie was saying.

The wasp looked angry. "I get it, you are a bit loony. I'll go easy on you when we begin the fight," he said.

"It's already on!" said Connie and jumped off the bee's back with a smirk. "This duel is fuelled by words!"

"Who are you and what farce are you turning this into?" asked the wasp and stiffened up ready for an attack.

"We are the Chauns and we want you to prove that what you said is true, or apologise and never bring it up again!" said Elma. "You might be stronger, but that doesn't mean that you are always right!"

"What?" snarled the wasp at her. "I'll sting you so badly your swollen head will swallow your fingertips and you'll look like a dumpling stuck on a—"

"Fork?" suggested the bee carefree. Elma chortled.

"Quiet!" bellowed the wasp. "Enough of this nonsense!"

"Look, we know you sting well, but you can't make honey can you?" asked Elma as she braved it and walked to the wasp. "Isn't that what your problem is? That you are no honey-boss."

"I can make honey!" cried the wasp.

"Again, prove it!" Connie said casually. "Tell us how you do it." The wasp didn't speak, but rather just stuttered embarrassed for a few long seconds before the bee cut in to save its crestfallen rival.

"Actually, wasps do help us make honey."

"Do they?" asked Elma stupefied.

"Yes, they help pollinate," explained the bee and the wasp looked at him with silent surprise. The bee must have known that wasps also frequently steal honey from them.

"There you go," Connie said. "No need to argue or fight! They can work side by side."

"Whatever," said the wasp. "You are all rather irritating and I'm sick of this now!" He flew off without saying goodbye.

"Don't worry, you are *so* much nicer," said Elma as she walked up to the bee to give him a tight, cosy hug.

"Oh no!" Lillian yelled and pointed at the sky. "The game! We are missing it!"

"Best not to tell Yeo everything about the trial," Connie said. "He'd play judge *all* the time!"

"He is going to be furious that we are late!" said Elma.

"And do what? Make biscuits from us?" laughed Connie. "There's every chance he is still waiting for everyone to return!"

"His take on the game did sound awful," Lillian commented gloomily.

They headed back to check but the whole group was there waiting for them. Yeo went for questioning them with the speed of a mousetrap snapping.

"There you are! You missed the whole thing! And what is this? You haven't even brought anything?"

"I did," Elma said and held out a strand of bee hair she had found fallen out earlier.

"As if anyone could ever find something like this!" yelled Yeo. "Simply unfit for purpose!"

"Oh, it's not meant to be hidden, I was going to give it to Hetty and Hammy."

The pair ran to her and examined the treasure. Hetty

rolled it up gently and Hammy put it in his big pocket.

"This is ridiculous," Yeo complained. "Connie, an explanation please!"

"Don't mind him," said Tuff. "He is upset because his game didn't go well."

"It did so!" Yeo scoffed.

"Can you prove it?" Connie asked laughing.

"Prove what?" Yeo asked bemused.

"Never mind," Lillian said. "We've heard enough arguments today! We stopped a bee from fighting a wasp and helped snails discover, during a tumultuous trial, that some of them clean their trails up!"

"How do they do that?" asked Yeo with sudden curiosity.

"Do what and who?" asked Lillian.

"Snails, how do they clean up?"

"I'm not sure, we didn't ask," said Lillian.

"But they don't have hands and they leave their goo as they go," said Yeo.

"They call it trodadoodle," Connie corrected him and the Duo booed Yeo for the lack of knowledge.

"That's a ridiculous thing to call it," Yeo defended himself. "Goo is perfect."

"Why, they do doodle with their trodadoole as they

trod on," commented Loch and Yeo sent him a long, hard look.

"Maybe they put a trailer on that cleans after them as they go," joked Anglo. "An eraser."

"That must be it," said Hammy.

"If anything, that's *not* it!" said Yeo angrily.

"It could be," said Lillian. "They clean so well that it leaves no marks apparently."

"How would they put a trailer on without hands?" asked Yeo. "I can't believe you didn't ask about this!"

"Why should we?" asked Connie. "Why would I ever need to know?"

"It's interesting!" retorted Yeo. "Like, they most likely drag along something under their body that wipes up as they go!"

"There you go, why ask if you have the answer," Connie commented. Yeo frowned.

"But it only raises more questions like what they use to wipe up with," he said.

"That's easy," said Elma. "Petals!"

"But how do—" began Yeo when at that moment, big fat raindrops started pelting the grass and the Chauns were quick to leap under a broad leaf for cover.

"Petals!" cried Hetty. "We should have just brought

our blankets to hide. They are all a different colour!" The group fell silent.

"We can still play then when we go back inside!" Yeo announced with triumph and the group fell silent. Hetty looked apologetic.

"Come on," Yeo urged them. "The rain isn't too heavy yet, we can make it back inside."

"Yes to go, no to play," said Anglo and Loch and dashed off first. Yeo ran after them making angry noises.

The others followed them back towards the terrace. But Connie stayed behind, looking at the hedge and thinking of the bee, and wondering what bees do when the weather turns bad. Tuff noticed Connie wasn't moving when he glanced back and came back to him.

"What's wrong?" he asked.

"Do you know what bees do when it rains?" Connie replied with another question.

"Can't say I do, sorry," said Tuff. "Why?"

"We met one earlier, before the snails," Connie explained. Then he thought of the snails and how they had two homes. Bees must have at least one then— their famous hive—he thought and felt better. Tuff looked at Connie's changing expressions with curiosity.

"Tell me all about it as we head back," said Tuff. And

so Connie did. He told Tuff about the wasp that mocked the bee and the two snails that had so much in common it became a problem.

"You've met lots of new faces," said Tuff. "I wish I were there too."

"I don't think the snails liked us though," Connie said smiling. "Your turn to tell me how did Yeo's game go wrong?"

"Well, we all came back with either sticks or tiny rocks," Tuff began. "But hiding those in the grass seemed silly and futile. So Yeo decided to pick a small bush in the garden, as fallen sticks and rocks aren't part of plants. He went first to hide his rock somewhere on the bush, and we looked away.

Then it was Anglo's turn, who found Yeo's rock as he was searching for a hiding place. So after him Yeo went up again, but he found Anglo's stick and became frustrated so in the end we just played regular hide–and–scare until you returned."

"He is lucky you guys returned," said Connie with a laugh. "He could've done with thinking about rules first."

"Sometimes the best way to find flaws is by doing something instead of thinking about it," Tuff said.

"Though, I do wish I went with you to meet the bee instead." And he began hopping as they reached the terrace, envisioning himself as the bee's coach right until they safely reached their bunk, saying:

"Shame there was no need to fight,
I could've taught him to punch right,
Here's a 'puff' and there's a 'bong',
It will surely sting for long!"

He jabbed a straight, then a curve,
He even had plenty in reserve.
Once you saw the strength he had,
to challenge him you must be mad.

He fought his way out of danger
Tough he was, the brave Chaun Ranger.
From each and every single match,
He emerged without a scratch.

That piece missing from his ear,
Wasn't from a foe to fear.
The culprit was none other,
The very hungry caterpillar.

Now no one would brag about
their ear mistaken for a sprout.
But he needed not to mention,
It caught everyone's attention.

They saw and said "Tuff prevails,
Him no injury ever derails!"
Tuff said "No, it's not a feat,
This scar comes from no defeat."

Well, it did look kind of cool,
Future foes it might just fool,
As a fine looking battle mark,
Whose owner is fearless of the dark.

Whilst most would always be in fear,
Of the risk of losing half an ear,
Today's ear-free honey bee
Would have made a good trainee.

The Lag

Distracted by his stories of yesteryear,
I suddenly realised the palace was near.
So immersed in his stories deep,
I jumped at a very fast, loud beep.

Horns blared and cars drove on,
The quiet streets of dawn were gone.
Oh I so enjoyed each story,
Of Hetty's skills and Tuff's glory.

But much to me was still unknown,
Like how he ended up alone.
I slowed down to cheat time,
As if I had steep hills to climb.

He took a sharp note of it,
And cried "We're lost, you must admit!"
I laughed and said "Please don't worry,
We're so very close, no need to hurry.

We are now on the right street,
Yet your story is incomplete.
Tell me how you lost your way,
Before farewells we have to say."

"Well, in the next story you'll learn
How events took such a turn.
But in short, before last night
We had a big, nasty fight.

I stormed off and climbed up a wall,
And sat there till rain came to fall.
But your Wacky Wind came too,
Without notice it blew and blew.

It caught me in a flimsy bag,
And so along I had to tag.
He flew us about with great joy,
Until a hedge seized his toy."

And so he ended up in Hyde Park,
Where alone he braved the dark.
Sitting on a fuchsia bloom,
He waited for daylight to resume.

And joys, I was the lucky one
To reach him just before the sun.
It was fate, only my nose
could've known his home was close.

When he said he lived on a frame,
Of a painting of a fine dame,
Located in a large room inside,
A place that tall furry hats guard,

I knew his home was not a shed,
But one ruled by a crowned head.
But you just wait until you hear
The final bits that are so near.

Banquet

Artificial light escaping through open windows disturbed the heavy darkness of the night in the palace gardens. The rooms adjacent to the White Drawing Room were full of life, hosting people dressed in elegant gowns and frocks, filling the room with laughter and chatter.

The complementing instrumental sounds crept out and ventured as far as they could, but were not strong enough to reach the trees, much to the relief of the hooting night owl.

The same could not be said about most of the Chauns. They lined up on their bunk, stuck, staring at the unbecoming occurrence in front of them.

"What is this!" Connie cried. "It's been on for hours!"

"I think it's a banquet," said Elma.

"I know it is,"—Connie looked grumpy and dangerously tired — "But it's outrageous! I can't sleep!"

"I'm sure it will be over soon," Lillian said trying to cheer him up.

"You reckon?" Connie asked doubtingly and pointed at a trolley of refreshments that was obviously recently filled to keep the guests and hosts content for longer.

"No hope for Connie to sleep," agreed Hammy as

well, and glumness sat on their face. They were very tired and upset. So moving somewhere else would have been not just difficult, but also very dangerous.

"I can still hear it even with my fingers jammed into my ears so deep they could almost scratch my eyeballs!" cried Connie as he took desperate measures to cut the noise out and now tried to roll and fold his ears to tuck them in but they popped out no matter how much force he used.

"How utterly awful!" he wailed and eyed Yeo for his headband as a potential remedy to keep his ears folded in place, but it was not on his head. This night was truly deplorable.

"Imagine how horrible Ninian must feel!" said Tuff. "I wonder where he is."

"Maybe his place is somewhere so amazing that he doesn't even hear this!" replied Connie, disinterested. "Given how much he hates noise I expect him to have chosen a quiet spot. Actually, let's go and find him and sleep there."

"I doubt it," said Tuff pensively. "He ought to be somewhere in this room, too."

"I thought he slept during the day and roamed around at night," said Loch. "Hence there's often stuff left out for us when we wake up."

"So we assume yes, but I wish he spoke!" said Yeo. "Then we would just know for sure."

"We know for sure that he likes to be alone," added Connie becoming increasingly irritable by the second.

"He is still part of our pack," Lillian reminded him, although she knew Connie was prone to being narky when tired; it was best to ignore him, albeit rather difficult.

The Duo started nudging and poking Yeo, indicating they wanted to make a move, for they were bored. Yeo looked at Connie wishing it was him the Duo nagged. Connie would have picked them up and laid them on the frame to roll them back and forth until they knew better than to poke him when he is tired. But the Duo already knew better than to tamper with Connie's inflamed mood and stuck to their favourite target—Yeo.

"We are not going anywhere," he said firmly to the mischievous pair. "It's too late, we are too tired and there are far too many people around!"

"Oo, oo, oouch oo!" they chimed and kept nudging him nonetheless. A quick cold shiver ran through Yeo for being criticised and yet he felt strangely ecstatic that they didn't brush him off with their usual response.

"Do excuse me for the too many 'toos'! It's very late, we are all tired, and there is an overwhelming number of people around!"

"Nay, nay!" laughed the Duo. Yeo gave a defeated sigh and looked around for help, but the others paid no attention. Connie was now sitting stiffly at the frame's edge, his chin sunk between his knees so that he could cast a constant evil glare at the people having fun, like a minuscule stupefied gargoyle.

Lillian was nearby, curling the ends of her ponytails around her fingers, and observing the crowds with genuine wishes for them to ebb away, whilst Elma was sitting in a lotus pose with her eyes closed, trying to block out the chatter and the laughs, or maybe just Connie's grumpy growling.

Loch and Anglo were rolled in their blankets, resting with their eyes closed. Hammy was patching a hole on Elma's belt and Hetty was mending Yeo's headband that had recently started to tear a little. Tuff was scanning the room hoping to spot Ninian by chance. The Duo were very bored and Yeo desperately tried to think of something to pass the time with, because as they waited time felt like it had been held back by colossal chains. Then gracious distraction struck with Lillian noticing something that made her run to Tuff at once.

"Tuff, look at the roses near the side door, can you see tiny golden flecks?"

Tuff scanned the area with a strong squint. Small they were and few in number, but they were indeed there, floating so slowly their silent motion was captivating.

"I think Connie has seen these before in the grass!" Lillian told him. "What do you think they could be?"

"I don't know," Tuff replied, still staring at them. "But I want to go and see."

"No, don't they might disappear like before, just please keep an eye on them whilst I tell Connie!"

And she ran back to him, knowing what Connie saw before was real and not a mirage.

"Connie!" she yelled even before she reached him. The gargoyle didn't move, only his eyes darted to the side, eyeing her with chilling suspicion.

"The golden flecks! They're here!" she rushed to say before Connie could crown his hostile moment with a growl. Connie's eyes widened with excitement and he jumped up eagerly. The lights were still in the same place when they reached Tuff, but as Connie began thinking of chasing them, they vanished like before. He froze instantly.

"Don't worry, I can see them again," Tuff said just before the last of Connie's excitement deserted him.

"Where?" he asked.

"At another bouquet, the pastel flowers in the far corner," said Tuff pointing. Indeed, they were now there, as if tiny glowing bees were searching for nectar. Elma had failed to block out any noise at all, so she heard everything and joined them as soon as Connie stood up.

Yeo also took interest in the matter and looked at the flecks in awe. The Duo followed him of course, but they were curious about the golden mystery too, and not just tailing Yeo. Loch and Anglo, however, kept stubbornly lying with their eyes shut.

"How could we go near it?" wondered Connie.

"Try calling it," said Hammy who was finished with Elma's ribbon and brought it over to her. She thanked him and tied it around her waist again.

"Hey, lights!" waved Connie and jumped with his arms stretched out. He tried to keep his voice at a reasonable level but the music was loud enough to keep them safe. The golden flecks didn't move, but something else near them did. Out from the mass of flower heads jumped Ninian.

"Ninian!" exclaimed Tuff happily. The solitary Chaun

was hopping around quickly and the golden flecks shifted, tailing after him.

"Oh, no!" cried Lillian. "Are they chasing him? What if they are malicious?"

The flecks were so beautiful, it was hard to imagine they could mean harm.

"Ninian! Watch out!" shouted Tuff having little faith that the distant Chaun would hear with the music being loud. But Ninian stopped and glanced at the painting, on top of which they stood, and smiled with a quick thumb-up. Then he carried on swiftly, heading towards them with the lights following. The sudden yell from Tuff was the final straw for Anglo and Loch. They gave up pretending that they were getting quality rest and went to see what was happening instead.

Hetty, who by now had also finished mending the headband, came with them. Ninian was quick and the lights that followed him suddenly became dimmer, so the Chauns had to keep a very close eye on them to keep track. Their eyes were following the loitering glows so closely that they jumped when Ninian's head suddenly appeared at the edge of the frame.

Because he roamed around alone at night when they slept, they forgot how fast Ninian was. He climbed up and waved to say hello.

The golden flecks slowly shifted to gather closely behind him, they looked very big close up, almost as big as Ninian's height, despite him being as tall as Anglo. He had kind eyes and regular Chaun ears with a pointy, rectangular finish to the top of his head and he wore a long cape, half of which was a huge pocket. A few ornamental details on his ensemble gave him a stately look.

"Ninian, what is going on?" asked Tuff. Ninian pointed at the golden floating balls first, then at Connie before placing his index finger under his left eye, where Connie had the small circular mark.

"They came to see me?" Ninian nodded and stepped aside. The glowing flecks drew closer.

"Wh-who are you?" asked Connie, a little scared.

"We are the flower sprites," said a soft, calming voice. Connie now looked truly startled.

"Look, we don't really mean to steal petals, we are big fans," he began and looked at his feet anxiously. "Big fans indeed, of the lovely texture and—" Just as he paused to find the right words, Anglo and Loch quickly tucked their petals away from sight. The sprites giggled softly.

"Don't worry, that's not why we came," they said. "We have been looking for you all since you went missing!"

"Missing?" asked Tuff, as Connie was speechless from the combination of relief and surprise. "From where?"

"From your home of course," said the soft voice.

"But we live here, we have lived here for a while now," explained Tuff and his head started to feel fuzzy.

"And before this?" asked the soft voice, but none of the Chauns had any recollection.

"We only know that we had fallen asleep in the Dark Float, and then woke up here, where there was light again," Lillian commented. They never wondered any more about what was before the new beginning, it felt like a start of it's own since they were all together. The sprites perhaps could see what she was thinking as they told them there were more of them at home.

"More Chauns?" asked Hammy overawed. "How can we not know that?"

"It has something to do with why you went missing," replied the sprites. "Or your tribe thinks it does at least."

"Wait," said Connie warily. "I have seen you before and you ran away from me!"

"We weren't sure if you were lost. We also had to identify the others too, so we have been observing you for a while, ever since we found you in the pot of roses."

"You were there too?" Connie asked.

"We are in all living flowers, across the world. But we can't leave and float around like this for long and we don't often do it so you normally can't see us."

Hammy and Hetty looked at the vast amount of flowers decorating the palace. "Are you in these ones too?" Hetty asked.

"No, these have been cut, they serve a different purpose. That's why it was lucky you came to the pot of roses, we had no idea you would be hiding inside a huge building somewhere!"

The Chauns felt very confused. Their heads were spinning from the new information that only gave root to an endless number of further questions.

"This sounds silly," Connie said suddenly.

"You are confused, it's understandable. But your desperate king asked us to find you, at the beginning of summer. You have been missing since the end of winter."

"We have a king?" asked Hammy, excited.

"Yes, and he is very worried about you, and the

prince," the sprites said.

"What prince?" asked Connie bemused. The sprites drew closer to Ninian.

"Ninian is a prince?" asked Tuff and felt bad for not knowing something so important.

"Yes, but something happened to him we think, for he can't talk. We might be able to treat him, flowers have some healing powers." The warming glow of the sprites suddenly went out and came back again—like a flickering bulb waving goodbye before burning out.

"Ay, he is not alone with that, these two dawdlers had a similar treatment," began Yeo as he pushed the Duo forward, prompting them to run and hide behind the group of Chauns.

"We will take a better look at this matter, but not now. We can't function for long this far from wild flowers. Come meet us at the gardens tomorrow, you will find us where the roses are growing."

"No! That's fooy, it's too far away," Anglo moaned. "It's the furthest possible place in the whole garden!"

But the sprites did not care and shot away with amazing speed, out the windows and into the darkness.

"Whoa, whoa, wait!" Hammy exclaimed. "Is this real?"

"I can't believe it!" Lillian cried.

"Did you know you are a prince?" she asked and looked at Ninian who shook his head vigorously.

"He couldn't have told us even if he did," said Loch. "It makes my head spin!"

"And other Chauns are looking for us and we had no idea," said Hammy.

"I bet they must be worried sick," Elma added.

"But Ninian has been right here all along to remind us and we still didn't remember that he is a prince," Tuff uttered with shock. "It's quite scary really."

"Yeo trying to boss us all around whilst Ninian should be in charge, it's funny if you ask us," said the Duo.

"Say what?" Yeo began fuming; his eyes grew larger with surprise before fury devoured every ounce of him. "Say? Say! You two devils! You cheating, nasty little freaks!"

The Duo laughed and gave each other a high five. Everybody else pretended to be astonished as well.

"What, they speak!" said Anglo, feigning shock that was far from believable. Yeo didn't buy it either and was so angry with everyone that he began to walk away, but Tuff stopped him.

"We need to stick together now," he said and looked

at Ninian who also agreed to stay with a nod. "You know what those two are like...."

But Yeo didn't. He felt like he knew nothing any more about his friends, their past and perhaps very scary future. His head felt tight and it made him angry.

"We are all in the same boat now, Yeo," said Lillian and sent an angry look at the Duo. "Was this really the right time?"

"Yes! Before those sprites break us trying to fix us!" Stoop retorted. "I could end up squeaking or something!"

"It would serve you well!" scoffed Yeo.

"Enough," began Connie. "Guys, this is serious."

"Yes," Elma said, "Let's not fight now."

The group fell silent and suddenly everything was quiet. With the shocking discovery completely distracting them they failed to notice that the banquet had ended. There was no movement in the room, no guests, just the lights kept on and fresh air flushing the rooms. Yet they didn't celebrate as sleeping no longer felt like a priority. Their heads were spinning and feeling heavy from everything they had heard.

"Does anyone know how we ended up here then?" Connie asked, but everyone shook their heads.

"We remember Yeo talking in his sleep," said the Duo. "It was torture."

"Is that why you have been making fun of me?" Yeo asked angrily but the Duo didn't answer him because it was very much the case that making fun of him was fun.

"How about you Ninian? Do you remember anything about the journey?" Tuff asked but Ninian shook his head again.

"Can you stay on our bunk tonight?" Lillian asked. "We should all go together tomorrow to find the flower sprites." Ninian nodded and put his hands together first, then to the side of his face and tilted his head slightly.

"He is right," Connie said rubbing his eyes. "Now that they have finally left we ought to get some rest."

They curled up in their petals and, contrary to their assumption they fell asleep quickly. Soon the lights were turned off, but the moon still danced with its reflection on the shiny surfaces, filling what it reached with a shallow night life. This was the time Ninian normally roamed around, but tonight—for the first night in a long time—he sat motionless, safeguarding the sleeping Chauns, and wondering what further changes the following day would bring.

The group woke early, just as palace staff entered to

tidy the room. But dusting had already been carried out the day before the banquet, so the Chauns felt safe on the frame.

"I dreamt ghosts took over the whole palace and chased us out!" cried Hammy.

"I had a bad dream, too! The palace vanished and we fell into a deep dark hole that was left in place of it!" said Hetty. "It was so awful!"

"I dreamt the opposite, we were tied to the bunk forever with yards and yards of sticky spider web," wailed Anglo.

"I also had a nightmare," said Elma.

"Me too," Loch added with a sour face and the Duo nodded. "Yeo did the nightmare note again, just for us..."

"And I dreamt I was stuck here with just you two forever," Yeo said, still sulking.

"Everyone seems to have had a nightmare but me," Connie said and the group looked at him as if he were trying to ruin the party.

"You probably just don't remember," began Lillian. "We must all be overwhelmed with the thought of potentially leaving."

"Potentially?" asked Anglo. "We will have to go

home, won't we?"

"I like it here," said Loch.

"Me too," added Connie. "This is home."

"But it might not be forever," Tuff reminded him.

"You mean it might disappear one day?" asked Elma. "Like in the nightmare?"

"No, just change it's purpose," explained Tuff. "Remember, we have no control of who does what to it."

"You mean," said Lillian. "Others would come and live in it instead of the current ginormees?"

"Nay, nay," said Yeo. "They would never leave the palace. They love it, so that would be preposterous!"

"I see you grew fond of the noodle language," said Connie and Yeo held his hand in front of his mouth, trying to shield away a faint cry of defeat.

"I didn't just say that!" he explained. "This is proof I *am* still in a nightmare!"

"Rusty says there are always people at the gates," Connie said. "It's a meaningful building."

"They're just checking it's still here," Yeo added importantly.

"We can wonder about it all we want, but it won't matter," said Tuff. "At any rate, the small but viable chance of change suggests we should leave."

"No," said Connie. "I like it here."

"But changed how?" asked Hetty. "It could become even more quiet instead of dangerous and then our bunk will be safe, moreover, there will be no banquets so that's ideal!" Connie nodded heavily.

"But Tuff has a point, it could turn into something bad," said Lillian. "A busy hotel, like the Ritz."

"Oh, who cares we have our own royals somewhere!" said Stoop. "Let's just go and see!"

"And there will be no more dust eaters!" added Stump. "Or dust whiskers!" They both began to jump around.

"And no more early mornings for Connie!" everyone said at the same time ending with a long laugh. Except for Connie, who didn't find it funny.

"Yeah laugh away but I don't do it on purpose!" he said annoyed. "And you should all be more careful about this whole discovery!"

Still, he was curious to hear more from the sprites, so they made sure everyone was ready and headed out when the room was left quiet and still. Although the group now looked at Ninian as the true leader who should go first, he shook his head and hands in protest so Tuff stepped forward instead. From parachuting to walking across the floor, they proceeded cautiously in single file, which made them look like a train of dust mites.

Outside was lovely and warm, with azure skies scrolling pompous white clouds. The rose garden was indeed a good distance away to the west, but the clear and wide paths gave an easy route for the Chauns to speed up significantly more than they could across the lawn. The dozens of flowerbeds gave home to many varieties of roses, and although their season was almost over, some defiantly beamed at eyes that might seek delight.

The Chauns approached one of the bushes with a red bloom and wondered if they should call out something, or call for someone. Except for Connie, who was—as always—strangely perplexed by the enormous Waterloo Vase nearby. He struggled to believe something so intimidating should be so near to the beautiful rose gardens, and despite it putting him off from approaching it, he felt like it was calling him with silent whispers.

"Chauns calling flower sprites," Anglo joked but nothing. He looked at Connie. "Maybe you should try, since they spoke to you."

Connie was still looking at the giant stone urn pensively.

"We came like you asked," he eventually said after a moment or two, but there was still no answer. He climbed up on the stalks and knocked on the green sepal. "Hello," he tried again, louder.

"Wait," came a scruffy voice. "We are getting ready."

Connie sent a confused expression to his friends and shrugged. Perhaps putting on a glowing coat was more time consuming than one would imagine. The golden flecks started to appear and float around them as he made his way back down.

"Sorry for the wait," said the soft voice this time. "It's a bit hard for us all to squeeze out of the last breath of a half-withered rose."

"Oh," Connie said. "I never would have thought of it that way."

"Not much longer until this gate is closed for the winter," the sprites explained. "We have a lot fewer resources during autumn so it's lucky we can deliver our promise to the Chaun King in time."

"The king again!" Lillian said. "Sorry, but this still sounds very new to us, maybe even dreamlike."

"A bad dream or a nightmare," Connie blurted out

and Lillian gave him a twinch telling him not to be rude.

"That hurt!" cried Connie. "I said nothing wrong!"

"We understand your frustration," came the reply. "Though we already told your king that we found you safe and well."

"Already? " Lillian asked. "What did he say?"

"He was relieved to hear you were safe," the soft voice said. "He said you must set off at once."

Connie didn't know what to say. After all, it wasn't even decided they would go.

"Why the rush?" he asked with furrowed brows.

"We don't know. The Chaun King came to us to ask for help but he is very secretive and he gives no explanation of his requests. We can't even tell you where they live."

"But you are everywhere! Surely you must have seen where they live?"

"We are where flowers are, but flowers are not everywhere," the sprites explained. "So we can tell you with certainty that while you don't dwell in flowers, your home is likely very far from here, based on where he summons us."

This sounded too mysterious, so Connie found it hard to believe and Loch was sceptical, too. The others, however, seemed ecstatic.

"This is so exciting!" cried Lillian. "A whole adventure and a secret location that we belong to!"

"I wonder where it could be!" Hetty cried. "I hope it's somewhere beautiful with lots of materials to use for attires!"

"Maybe we can have a room just for our finds and no one will remove it if it's left unattended," Hammy said with a coy smile. "Quick! Tell us where to go!"

"Hang on," said Connie. "Let's think this through first."

"Yes," Loch agreed. "Why should we barge into the unknown? Can they be trusted?"

"They might not be kind and this supposed journey may be long and very dangerous, with not more Chauns in the end but grave perils instead," Connie posited.

But Elma had her focus elsewhere. "They come from flowers, pretty flowers. What harm could they mean?"

"Actually," began Yeo. "Have you heard of poison ivy? It has a rather descriptive name."

"Aren't those plants?" asked Hammy

"Some plants bloom," said the soft voice tensely. "And when they do, we are present at poison ivies too."

"Although that doesn't mean we deliver harm," added the scruffy voice.

"Of course," said the Duo trying to keep a serious face whilst eyeing Yeo. "Wasn't that rude of him to suggest!"

"Excuse me," said Yeo with an angry tone. "I never once suggested that they did so."

"You did kind of imply that they were lying," said Anglo jokingly. "It's no better."

"It wasn't me," Yeo said. "That was Connie!"

"Stop it, all of you," Lillian said. "Why would they lie?"

"Yes, surely they must know that lying is bad," Elma joined in.

"Forgive us for a moment," Connie said and held his hand up towards the sprites as he looked at Lillian and Elma. "Might I remind you two that *anyone* can lie in general?"

"No, not me," Lillian said and turned her nose up with a sulk.

"Me either," Elma said siding with Lillian as she crossed her arms in protest.

"Never! We don't lie," insisted Hetty. "Have you forgotten why?"

"No, I didn't, so don't—" began Connie but he couldn't stop them reminding him.

"Never lie, for lying is bad,
And when you're busted it makes you sad,
thinking oh why am I not clever
enough to make lies that are better?
But if I were so good, I could just cheat,
no one would know, I'd lie I was neat.
I might even steal and when they look
I'd be the first one to find the crook.
I'd point at the closest fishy face,
crush their excuse at lightning pace.
"You say that you were out at sea?
I saw you weren't, don't lie to me!"
Cos' lying is for those that can
convince a cock that he's a hen.
It's the deal of life a tongue so sleek,
It supplies endless lies to leak.
Lies that can then turn a face stiff
Making the lies harder to sniff.
A total win, called poker face,
It has no shame and knows no grace.
Who cares that the heart might rot
When *all* could be fooled, not just a tot!
But no, not me, I never will
My soul can't handle all the thrill,

For I couldn't lie more than once till,

I had to face it: trying is futile.

It's true and I will never know why

My face can't hide a single lie.

But lying is bad, I should rejoice—

the world echoes my honest voice,

Saying life is sour and dull

Once you already traded your soul,

So never lie for lying is bad..."

"Hang on!" Yeo cried. "Liars! You are lying about never lying because you didn't tell me about the Duo's nasty deceit!"

"We tried," began Connie. "But you—"

"Forget it," Anglo said. "If you never asked, it's all your fault."

"Yes," the Duo said. "We don't accept complaints. That would be *postrous.*"

Anger took a shot at Yeo's face, hitting it hard as he flailed his arms at them rabidly.

"Stop it!" Connie cried. "We have more important things to focus on!" He looked at the sprites, who were loosely hovering around Ninian, and pointed an accusing finger.

"You said you weren't sure I was a lost Chaun when you first saw me. But on that particular day I was very much lost, locked in a flower wrap." Connie eyed the sprites with glee. He was proud of his approach to bust their credibility.

"You were sniffing the petals and rubbing them on your skin, before using the leaves as a trampoline. You looked like you were having an awful lot of fun until you became trapped."

The group looked at Connie.

"What?" he muttered. "We often bounce on large petals and sturdy leaves, it's fun." He looked at Hetty

and Hammy to seek support, for those two loved bouncing just as much as he did, but they seemed strangely fascinated by the rose stalks all of a sudden.

"So you wanted to go alone to have the whole miniature playground for yourself?" asked Lillian. "Did you lose the bet on purpose?"

"No, I only went for a petal," Connie said fiercely. "It could be that I stayed there playing a bit longer than I should have, or it could be that this is just another nonsense from the sprites to stir up a fight between us."

Lillian sighed. "You can't lie either, Connie," she said.

"It's written on your face, like the lie note warns," Elma reminded him.

"Shh!" Tuff suddenly silenced them and they all noticed that the sprites now surrounded Ninian tightly, having ignored the Chaun argument completely. They still moved slowly around him, but soon they sped up and as they did, they turned into a blurry picture of spiralling lights that rapidly became painfully fast to watch. The Chauns squinted and drew their palms to shield their eyes. But Ninian stood in the centre peacefully, his eyes gently closed.

"What have you done to him?" Connie cried with

horror when he heard the fuzzing noises stop.

"We scanned him to see what was wrong with him," the scruffy voice said. "All I can say to your distrust is that we are part of an environment that creates, and encourages animated and aesthetic balance. You need not be afraid of us."

"So you fixed him?" Tuff asked eagerly.

"No," the scruffy voice said with a hint of sorrow. "Something sinister caused this."

"Something sinister?" Elma cried with fear. "You mean evil?"

"We fear it may be a jinx," the scruffy voice explained. "Which could be a good sign if it's a reversible one. But what we tried to reverse it was not successful so you must try to find the cure because it is still taking effect on him."

"No!" Tuff and Lillian yelled at the same time.

"Don't be ridiculous," Connie said. "He looks fine!"

"This jinx is deep inside him and not on the surface. Herbs and flowers have strong healing properties, but this evil goes beyond their realm," said the soft voice. "You really should go back and see if the king has better knowledge about what could have caused this. He may recognise it when he sees it, for his knowledge is superlative. He even knew how to summon us."

"Where do we go to meet him?" asked Tuff desperately.

"I can't tell you yet," replied the soft voice.

"Why not?" Yeo asked, gobsmacked. "You finally found us and you won't say?"

"We were instructed to only hand over the information once you are all ready to go. You are not in complete agreement."

"We all will go, we can tie Connie and Loch to our backs!" Lillian pleaded.

"No," the scruffy voice said sternly. "Go, think about it and get ready. Come and find us here again tomorrow. But be warned, that will be your last chance. The fewer gates we have the less we want to venture."

"You are kidding, right?" cried Anglo. "At least pick a closer place to the palace!"

"You can come out here again," said the scruffy voice sternly. "And when your king calls us today I will ask for his permission to pass the information to you regardless of your stance tomorrow. We are tired of this task now and would prefer if the king's daily calls for updates stopped, too."

And with that, the sprites drew back into the roses to

disappear through invisible gates.

"Look at what you two have done!" cried Yeo looking at Connie and Loch. "It's all your fault!"

"Yes, poor Ninian is suffering and we lost a whole day because of you," Tuff yelled angrily, which was unusual for him to do.

"Connie," said Lillian. "There is no reason not to believe the sprites! They knew Ninian couldn't speak!"

"You ask a question from him and he doesn't reply," Connie said vehemently. "It's not hard to reach that conclusion!"

"Those in favour of going should stick their hands up," said Tuff and everyone apart from Connie did so. Even Loch.

"Oh come on," cried Connie. "You too, Loch? If ever, you should be in doubt *now*!"

"We are going to convince the sprites tomorrow even if you are not with us," Lillian warned him with sad eyes. "We are leaving tomorrow."

"Suit yourself," Connie said sulkily as he turned away. "I just struggle to believe them, I can't help it. They might tell you even if I am not there."

"I know you like it here," Tuff said kindly. "But there's every chance you'll like our original home more."

"Don't you secretly wish for somewhere we truly belong?" Hetty asked.

"It makes sense that we belong somewhere else," Hammy added. "It's actually really fortunate that we do so."

"I'm not coming back to the bunk tonight," Connie began. "See how you like change. Then we will talk about it more tomorrow."

"There is nothing to talk about Connie, we simply must go! Even if there is a slight risk we have to try for Ninian's sake!" Lillian pleaded.

"Slight!" Connie snorted and shook his hands vigorously. "Like I said, think about it!" And as he held

up a warning index finger, he began to stomp off.

"You better meet us here at noon tomorrow!" Lillian yelled after him, with worry and sadness inciting her tone more than anger.

Huffing and puffing, Connie stuck to his guns with pure force of will and no logic. He wasn't sure why he felt so strongly about this, but it brought back uncomfortable sensations similar to just after the Dark Float and it made him feel truly uneasy. He walked until he faced a wall and climbed up on it, where—as you already know—he was caught by the wind and flown to Hyde Park overnight. Having not much better to do, he thought and thought and thought some more.

> To go or not that is the question,
> To decide what to do we need to mention,
> A few things about the route,
> That would even daunt a brute.
>
> So why should we, just tiny flecks
> Charge west through thick forests?
> When high up we safely roam
> And endless flowers are for loan.

Don't be silly and tell us to go,

Our progress would be nothing but slow.

By the time we'd make it there,

We would have walked ourselves bare.

Meanwhile in this cosy palace,

Shielded strong from spite and malice,

We could just play, have fun all day,

The thought might make us weep, far away.

I wonder if it's true at all,

Or if they just like to trick the small.

We could end up in a lost land,

Or be swallowed by quicksand.

Oh the horrors, the risk is real,

Once we're gone our bunk they'll steal.

But since they'll go, so shall I,

For they will need a guarding eye.

Still, I worry, I'll tell you why,

With no face to show a lie,

There's no risk of being busted,

Hence I say they can't be trusted!

Bon Voyage

"Take a bird," I said, "Why not?
They fly long distance a lot."
He said, "It's only Rusty we trust;
her name is not for red, but for rust.

She is now old and lives tired days,
So in the garden is where she stays.
And however hard she tries,
her bones all ache whenever she flies."

"I could send you by Royal Mail,
Their special post will never fail
To send you where you truly belong,
Signed for by the 1pm gong."

"But do they go to Chaun Kingdom,
At pine millionth over the Somme?
Far beyond cold hills and tall trees
Where no one can venture with any ease?"

(Of course he said a fake address
the real one could never be guessed;
Though I think I'll take my chance
To assume it's not in France.)

I said "Guess not, it is a shame,
You'll have to walk all the same.
Had they told you your destination
I could've helped with your migration.

But this secret is of import,
Leaking it could bring danger forth.
Still, I don't think it's a trap,
Something had to cause your nap.

Once you find out, you *can* come back,
And along with you bring the whole pack!
Since it's guarded against all malice
back doors guide you in the palace."

"Thanks," he said as I stopped by the wall,
I couldn't reach up, it was too tall.
But he climbed it fast and very steady,
I felt quite sad to part already.

I looked away, scanning the ground
as if I was somewhat spellbound.
We said no goodbye yet when I
Let out a loud and sudden cry,

"Wait, this is not good for my heart,
to hear no news of you once we part.
Not knowing what lies ahead,
Will drive me completely mad, I dread!"

"I guess," I heard him loudly say,
"We could maybe find a way.
But for me to message you,
We will need a thing or two.

Buy a pot of flowers and,
if the sprites give me a hand,
They will visit you at night;
But they won't show you their light.

You will be asleep when we meet,
Through my words, which the sprites repeat.
Unreal as it maybe seems,
There is a world inside your dreams."

"But can they find me with their powers?
Many rooms have potted flowers."
"Well, could you have something rare,
Something that's not everywhere?"

"I could have three orchids aligned,
All plain yellow, so easy to find.
And if needs be, to keep their bloom
I'll grow a jungle in my room."

He chuckled and he yelled "OK,
Just make sure it's not a bouquet!"
Being back now, his spell grew stronger
To look for him I could no longer.

"Bye!" I heard; I waved at the wall,
It was now over once and for all.
He had to go and I had to wait,
For sprites to use my orchid gate.

The gate I didn't have yet so I,
Ran to the nearest florist to buy
three yellow orchids that,
I could re-house in my flat.

As I briskly walked I thought
Of the same dilemma that he fought,
When he asked if the sprites had lied,
And he could not pick a side.

He just feared for the worst,
And could not dive head-first
Into a trip that could be fake,
When he knew how much was at stake.

Doubts in my head started to wake
I, too, had a lot at stake.
If the sprites were indeed grim,
I would never hear from him.

And never is a long time to wait,
and wait and wait and wait,
And wait and wait and wait.
But wait! How long one can wait?

It could go on forever at this rate!
And what if Big Wait itself is late?
It'd just add to the wait—
When waiting I already hate!

But since there is some good in most bad,
if the long wait drove me mad,
Life could still be great and grand,
in this place called Wonderland.

With that thought I had made up my mind—
the prettiest orchids I would find!
And I would *not* lose my hope before,
All sprites had heard my snore!

Printed in Great
Britain
by Amazon